"Hazel!" The baritone sound of his voice now heated her blood. What was that? Whatever it was, it would disappear. It had to.

In less than sixteen hours, she was going to walk back through the hospital doors. She truly hadn't expected to see Syver. Part of her had hoped. But working with him? She'd never let herself hope for that.

The looks he gave her reminded her that their connection, the easy one they had, still simmered beneath the years and distance. If it was that obvious, better to address it before they worked their first shift.

Turning, she bit her lip to keep the smile her brain wanted to form from appearing. She was lonely. It had been a rough few years, and her soul wanted to jump into friendship. To recover something she'd thought lost forever.

But she wasn't the naive woman she'd been. Hazel faced conflict now. Addressed issues. Truth might hurt, but it was better than a fantasy.

Crossing her arms, she waited for him to reach her. Had he always been so tall…so handsome?

Yes.

Dear Reader,

When I first started *Tempted by Her Royal Best Friend*, I had Hazel pictured perfectly in my mind. Sometimes a character just comes to you. What I didn't count on was how writing her other half, Prince Syver, would make me ache for him. He's the hero we all deserve; he just can't see it in himself.

Nurse Hazel Simpson grew up knowing she was unwanted. Even her name was based on the color of her eyes. But she's finally stepping out on her own. The island kingdom of Fönn is her new start!

Prince Syver is the doctor prince. The man who left Fönn—at least that is the official story. So much more palatable than his family banishing him. They recalled him after he finished his residency, and he has spent the past five years doing his best to make them happy. And falling short each time. But now Hazel has arrived. His former best friend, the woman he cared for, who knew the real him.

Giving these two characters their happily-ever-after was fun and exciting. I hope you find their path to love as satisfying as I do.

Juliette

TEMPTED BY HER
ROYAL BEST FRIEND

———

JULIETTE HYLAND

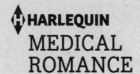

HARLEQUIN
MEDICAL
ROMANCE

Recycling programs
for this product may
not exist in your area.

ISBN-13: 978-1-335-73791-5

Tempted by Her Royal Best Friend

Copyright © 2023 by Juliette Hyland

For questions and comments about the quality of this book,
please contact us at CustomerService@Harlequin.com.

Harlequin Enterprises ULC
22 Adelaide St. West, 41st Floor
Toronto, Ontario M5H 4E3, Canada
www.Harlequin.com

Printed in U.S.A.

Juliette Hyland began crafting heroes and heroines in high school. She lives in Ohio with her Prince Charming, who has patiently listened to many rants regarding characters failing to follow the outline. When not working on fun and flirty happily-ever-afters, Juliette can be found spending time with her beautiful daughters, giant dogs or sewing uneven stitches with her sewing machine.

Books by Juliette Hyland

Harlequin Medical Romance

Neonatal Nurses

A Nurse to Claim His Heart

Falling Again for the Single Dad
A Stolen Kiss with the Midwife
The Pediatrician's Twin Bombshell
Reawakened at the South Pole
The Vet's Unexpected Houseguest
The Prince's One-Night Baby
Rules of Their Fake Florida Fling
Redeeming Her Hot-Shot Vet

Visit the Author Profile page at Harlequin.com.

For all the people who've made tough choices
for the sake of their own well-being. You are seen.

PROLOGUE

THE NEXT SHIFT was arriving at London Pediatric Hospital, and Dr. Syver Bernhardt strained his neck, looking for the mess of dark curls.

"You ready, Dr. Bernhardt?"

Syver didn't even attempt to hide his smile as he turned to find nurse Hazel Simpson behind him. "You got me."

"'Bout time!" She clapped her hands and tapped his arm with hers. "I think the current score is Hazel three, Syver five hundred!"

"You've won over three times." It had to be at least ten. Though she was right, this was one thing he took first place in!

"And you've won more than five hundred."

It was a silly game. One he didn't even remember the origins of. Somehow, he'd snuck up on her when they were on opposite shifts to say good morning… or was it good evening? It didn't matter. The game of being first to greet the other had stuck, and he was the reigning champion.

"You'll catch up one day!" He followed her into the staff room, grabbing his backpack as she placed hers in a locker.

"I doubt it. But I don't need to catch up."

This really was the perfect way to begin or end a shift. Hazel was his best friend, roommate and colleague. He saw her constantly and yet never tired of their inside jokes.

Her nose twitched, and he knew she was about to press a point. "You didn't answer my question, though. You ready to be an attending?"

"Yes…and no." He slung his backpack over his shoulder, wishing he sounded surer of himself. He was excited, ready to finish his residency. Prepared to take on medicine as a full pediatrician. No more student physician, intern or residency. He'd completed today's shift, so technically, he was an attending physician.

It seemed like he'd been in med school, internship and residency for half his life. Which wasn't that far off!

This was his dream. The one he'd set for himself when his old life vanished. The goal that let him reach for something that wasn't home. Or the family he'd been cast out of.

For the first time in his life, he'd truly felt like himself. The real Syver, the one no one wanted to know at home, had flourished here.

He'd trained to be a pediatrician, thought of little else besides that goal. Now the day was arriving. He was reaching his end point.

Now he was Dr. Bernhardt, attending pediatrician. And part of him wondered if he was really ready. If he'd learned enough. If he'd be good enough.

"I felt the same way when I finished nursing

school. Ready, *and not*, excited, and a tad terrified. All normal reactions. You're ready, Syver. And we are celebrating as soon as I get home!"

Hazel ran her hand along his shoulder, the connection brief...and friendly. That is what they were, friends and roommates. She'd moved into his flat two years ago, after her roommate's marriage. What was supposed to be a temporary arrangement had flourished into a friendship he'd never expected.

"Movies, popcorn and takeaway!" A Saturday tradition, at least when they were both free.

Hazel tilted her head, her bright eyes meeting his. "If you want to actually go out, we can. Someplace fancy, even. You've certainly earned it." Then she followed him out of the staff lounge and grabbed a tablet chart off the charger.

"And mess with tradition! No way." He'd spent his childhood going to fancy parties, elite restaurants, stuffed into suits and told to stay quiet.

He'd spent years playing a role he never quite fit. There was something special about spending time with a dear friend. Relaxing in confines of your home with no expectations.

And that time was always better when Hazel was by his side.

Besides, she was working the night shift. Even after a few hours of sleep, Hazel would prefer to slip into comfy pants and crash on the couch. And that was where he wanted to be, too. An epic celebration was epic just because they were having fun together. The location didn't matter.

"All right, if you're sure. I need to do patient transfers, but I put a lemon cookie on the counter for you."

"Best roommate ever!" Syver raised a hand as he headed for the door. "Good job sneaking up on me today, but come Monday…"

"Yeah…yeah!" Hazel waved and then turned toward the nursing station.

Syver whistled as he walked up the stairs to their flat. The Tube wasn't very crowded, and he'd hit the station at just the right time. He was officially Dr. Bernhardt and the life he'd carved out for himself was truly taking root.

"Your Highness."

He wasn't sure how the security service had entered his apartment, but Syver didn't care.

He was finally just Syver. Not Your Royal Highness, not Prince. Just Syver. It had taken years to settle into that. Years to accept that the royal family of Fönn preferred him forgotten.

"That isn't a title I answer to." *Not anymore.*

He'd been officially, but secretly, banished as soon as he turned eighteen. The King would never admit his queen had cheated. People suspected, there'd even been a few "news" articles, all quickly hushed up, but it was not discussed. Though the King never hid his distaste for his "second" son.

They only thing he'd ever done to please the King was leave.

That was a wound buried so deep in his soul, Syver didn't think it would ever stop weeping.

Dropping his backpack, he stepped into the living room, stunned to see three guards in Fönn regalia standing in formation. "What are you doing here? I've not broken any of the King's rules."

He'd maintained a low profile; no one knew his origins. He'd studied at university, invested the payment the kingdom had given him and kept to himself. There was no reason for the guard to be in his home.

A look passed between the well-trained guards. The world teetered as the air in the room shifted. "What is going on?"

"The King requests you return home."

He couldn't stop the laugh, though there was no humor in the chuckle. "You're going to have to do better than that. After all, it's the King who sent me away."

And told me I was never to set foot back in the kingdom.

That second part wasn't exactly public knowledge, but it didn't surprise him that the security personnel didn't react. Either they were very skilled at their jobs, a distinct possibility, or it wasn't news to them. Maybe both.

"King Eirvin passed this morning."

The security officers parted, then bo

Syver's brother stepped up. "It's *me* who requires you at home."

His brother's presence stole the wind from Syver's planned responses. The King was dead. The man everyone in Fönn assumed was Syver's father. The man who'd told him he was no longer part of the family was gone.

There were emotions he should feel. Anger, sadness…relief. But nothing came. The news settled like a lead balloon in the room as he tried to process the information. Tried to react.

"You're the last person I expected to see here. Shouldn't you be getting ready for a coronation?" The words lacked the deference he'd been trained to give his brother, but Erik didn't flinch.

"I doubted you'd come if I sent just the guard. Personal touch and all."

Personal touch. The words sounded liked they tasted bad. There was little hint of personal in this.

He came. For me.

No one had come for Syver…ever.

"The Dowager Queen hasn't stopped crying. She also wishes for your return."

Dowager Queen? Why didn't Erik ever call her mum? Titles, propriety, it all came first…and Syver always fell short.

Mum. His heart swelled, then crashed with worry. Was she all right? Probably not. Though he doubted she'd ever show it. But she wanted him home.

Words he'd never expected to hear made his heart soar. His family wanted him.

As if summoned by Erik's words, his mobile rang. "Mum…" She was calling. Calling him.

Syver took a deep breath as he looked around the flat. He'd called this place home for almost ten years. He'd mourned home, hated his banishment for the first year. Now the idea of leaving hurt, too.

"I need you, Syver, Erik needs you, Fönn… well, Fönn needs you, too." Pauses punctuated her words, and he could hear the tears in her voice. King Eirvin had cheated on the Queen regularly, but she'd loved him through it all. The one time she'd fallen for another…well, that had resulted in Syver. King Eirvin had not been as forgiving as his queen.

But if they needed him, wanted him, Syver would come.

"I'll be on my way shortly. I need to finish up a few things here—"

Hazel…

They were celebrating and the idea of leaving her. His throat closed. Maybe she'd like a change of location? The idea of not seeing her again, of not living with her…

"Sorry, Your Highness." The guard's tense words broke through his pained musings. "Our orders are to depart as soon as you have a bag packed."

Your Highness. It took him a moment to realize they were speaking to him, not his brother.

"My presence in England is unknown. And must remain that way. The funeral is tomorrow and then my coronation. You are the heir to the throne." Erik's words were firm, already king-like.

Heir to the throne, a throne he had no right to, and didn't want.

"Fönn needs doctors and a united royal family. You're part of Fönn's future."

Part of Fönn's future.

He'd see the frozen shores, attend the Summer Nights Festival, be part of the family he'd been thrown out of. It was a dream he'd given up when he'd landed in London, one he'd convinced himself he no longer wanted.

He closed his eyes and said a soft goodbye to the life he had here.

"Mum, I need to say goodbye…"

"There isn't time, Syver. You must come now. It is not fair, but it is the role of a prince. Fönn needs you." Her words were soft, but he heard the bite of the Queen behind them. Duty first. He might not have King Eirvin's blood flowing through him, but he'd been raised as a prince.

Forever duty. There were sacrifices to be made, but home and family—he couldn't say no.

His throat closed as he felt the royal mask slip back on. He'd sworn when he'd left Fönn that he'd not step foot back on its shores.

But that didn't mean he didn't yearn for it.

"I'll see you soon." A promise he could finally

keep. He heard his mother sigh before she whispered a goodbye.

He slid the phone back into his pocket and walked into the kitchen. The sight of the cookie pulled another lump into his throat. He'd not told his best friend who he was. It wasn't supposed to matter, didn't matter when he was here.

In London he was Dr. Syver Bernhardt. It was a role he loved, the one he'd found solace in when his world was so empty.

But it hadn't been empty after he'd met Hazel. He was her silly best friend. A woman who saw him as he saw himself...perhaps the only person in the world who knew the private man.

He'd not wanted to lose that. Not wanted to see the shift if she learned he was royalty. *Even cast-out royalty.*

That selfish decision now meant she was going to come home to an empty flat and a truth he wouldn't be here to share personally.

It was time to go home, but he'd find a way to get back to Hazel. Someway.

For now, she was safe and secure. That was what mattered. He owned the London flat, and she could stay as long as she wanted.

Forever.

The word slid into his mind, but he pushed it out. He needed to focus on his family for the moment, but he also needed her to know she was part of it, too.

Pulling a note from the drawer, he stared at the blank lines. How did one write *goodbye, I'm sorry* and *give me a few months to figure things out* in one short missive?

"We need to get moving, Syver." Erik's words were sharp as Syver heard security tossing things into boxes in his room.

In the end, he scratched out a few words he knew weren't enough. He'd make it up to her as soon as he resettled in Fönn.

CHAPTER ONE

Five years later

THE NORDIC ISLAND KINGDOM of Fönn was barely visible through the chilly fog, but Hazel Simpson could just make out the outline of the shore. At least she thought it was the shore.

Pulling into the heavy coat, she stared at her new home. The travel nursing contract let her work in Fönn for the next twelve months, though the nursing contractor let her know the kingdom was very interested in those taking contracts staying on.

Would they be if they knew my history?

She closed her eyes, pushing the unwelcome thought away. It wasn't her history. Not really.

Not that anyone in London cared. People who'd known her. People who claimed to be her friends had turned their back in her darkest moment. Her mother, who'd finally reconnected with her, had walked away. Calling her a naive idiot who ruined everything.

She'd accepted that the life she'd known, even if it wasn't a fairy tale, was over.

Alec had led her on for three years. Three years of playing the perfect girlfriend at investment events, of hiding her unhappiness, hoping that things would change. Three years of accepting expensive gifts when he missed a date, or anniversary or was a giant jerk. Three years of not asking enough questions. Three years accepting the bare minimum in a relationship. Three years with a con man whose company was nothing more than a Ponzi scheme.

Three years of her life down the drain. And with it, the career she'd built.

She had known nothing about Alec's crimes. The National Crime Agency cleared her. Though the investigator mentioned it shocked him how blind she'd been as he carted the expensive jewelry and electronics from her flat.

Items she hadn't wanted…not that anyone believed her. No. They thought she loved the fancy life Alec provided. When they'd met, he'd been a penniless stockbroker, then he'd hit it big…or at least that was what he'd told her.

And she'd wanted to believe him. Wanted to think that this was the person who wanted to be with her. The person who finally loved her for her.

Naive. She'd been so naive.

Her colleagues didn't agree with the assessment. They didn't think you could live with someone and not know them. *Twice.*

That was the real rub. She'd lived with a man she hadn't truly known twice.

Prince Syver Bernhardt.

Her onetime roommate and best friend. And the heir to the throne of the island nation where her ferry would land in a little over an hour.

Five years ago, she'd protested. She hadn't known. Like the rest of the hospital, the rest of London, it was shocking to find that a prince resided unknown among them.

No one had realized royalty from the tiny nation was sitting beside them. Working with them, acting like one of them. He'd buried that truth so well.

Or maybe she just hadn't dug deep enough. Maybe, like with Alec, the signs had been there, and she'd ignored them. It was so easy to believe a pretty lie.

The note Syver left on the counter with the cookie she'd gotten him was less than half a page. A quick goodbye, a promise she could stay in the flat as long as she needed.

Like she wanted to be there without him.

Yet it was one of the few possessions she'd brought with her.

Why?

That was a question that had bounced around her brain each time she boxed up her life. And she had no better answer today than she did when she packed up their flat.

His flat.

Syver owned the flat. Something she should have picked up on. He hadn't cared about her rent, hadn't charged her market price. Another clue she'd ignored because she'd craved stability.

Searching for that stability, grasping for it, clinging to mirages of it, had only caused her pain.

"Careful, Elias!" a woman called as a little boy darted past Hazel.

The child laughed as he raced to the railing.

Hazel's stomach jumped to her throat as the boy reached over the railing, his mother stepping to his side. The child was fine, just enjoying the boat ride.

As a pediatric nurse-practitioner, she'd seen more fall injuries and broken bones in children than she could count.

He laughed and his mother stroked her son's head. Such a simple motion, one Hazel had never experienced. Her mother didn't know the definition of affectionate.

Hell, the woman hadn't wanted her. Maybe another would have hidden that dark secret, not Rita Simpson. She'd made sure Hazel knew from the time she was old enough to understand that she was an unwanted drain on her mother's life and purse. Even her name, Hazel, was after the color of her eyes. And only given after the nurse said she had to have a name to exit the hospital.

Leaning against the railing, Hazel kept her eyes from the young family. Focus on the future. On Fönn.

She bit her lip as the image of Syver danced in her memory. He would have believed she didn't know about Alec's schemes. He'd have listened.

But he wasn't there. He'd left her and never looked back.

He's where I'm going.

Fönn. Where Syver was the heir to the throne. The island nation had expected King Erik and his wife to have a child as soon as they wed. Three years later, the island was still waiting.

Most of London had stopped following the tiny island politics after watching Syver stand in the audience of his brother's coronation.

Not Hazel.

She knew he dated aristocratic women who graced magazine covers. Long blond hair, crystal-blue eyes with legs for ages.

Never for very long, just long enough to get local bloggers hoping he might settle down. The women were her polar opposite, in looks and status.

Not that it mattered. They'd only ever been friends.

Best friends.

Or were they? Friends didn't keep such secrets.

Water under the bridge, Hazel. It wasn't like she'd see him. The blogs and articles referred to him as the doctor heir, but never mentioned him working in medicine. Royal life wasn't exactly designed for a full-time job.

Which was a shame. Syver was a gifted pediatrician, one of the best she'd worked with in her nursing career. But what role did medicine have to play when you wore a crown?

A screech echoed over the boat's engines, and Hazel instinctively turned toward the boy she'd seen earlier. But he was safe in his mother's arms.

The cries came again, echoing from the back of the boat. An accident, and as a nurse, she knew her place. So she made her way toward the commotion. It didn't take long for an announcement to echo over the intercom.

"Is there a doctor on board? If so, please come to the back of the boat immediately."

Hazel wasn't a physician, but she knew the cries of an injured child.

She moved as fast as was safe on the wet deck. A small gathering was accumulating around the injured, and she pushed her way through. "I'm a nurse."

The little girl was sitting in her mother's lap, tears racing down her cheeks as she cradled her left arm.

"It hurts!" The wail broke Hazel's heart as she knelt beside the little one.

"I'm Hazel, a nurse." She smiled at the young girl, then looked at her mother. No other medical professionals stepped forward, but fortunately, and unfortunately for the child, it didn't take a doctor to diagnose the issue at hand.

Her wrist was already two times the size it should be, and bruises were popping up. Broken.

How bad? Only an X-ray could determine that, but the child was going to be in pain until they could get her treated.

"I need you," Hazel pointed to a man standing in the circle of gawkers, "to let the captain know we have a broken wrist. I need transport to the children's hospital available when we arrive. And ask how long it will take for us to reach the dock."

She didn't add *please*; this was an order. In emergency situations, directing someone to do something was better than asking.

Hazel pointed to a woman. "I need you to get me a first aid kit." She'd seen two white boxes with red crosses attached to the wall. Inside should be an instant ice pack, gauze and something she could use to stabilize the wrist.

The woman took off and was back before long, her face dejected. "This was all that was in them." The woman held up what looked like dirty gauze and two packs of Band-Aids.

Hazel looked at the poor offering and made a mental note to make sure she mentioned they needed restocking. But that was a problem for another day.

"All right then, find me a board, or anything sturdy I can use to stabilize her wrist. And ask the captain if he has ice somewhere."

The woman took off, and Hazel pushed the hood of her parka back. A little water slipped into her jumper, and Hazel shivered as she looked at the girl. "Can you tell me your name?"

"Ebba." The little girl sniffed, shifted in her mum's lap, then let out another sob.

"I know it's hard, Ebba, but I need you to stay as still as possible. Okay?"

"We have twenty minutes before landfall." The man she'd sent to talk to the captain coughed as he slid to a stop, barely catching himself.

Thank goodness. Hazel didn't need to add to her patient list.

"There will be transportation to take you to hospital. He didn't call for a medic, though."

"That's fine." Hazel nodded. The broken arm was an emergency but didn't require a medic or ambulance transport.

"This is all I could find." The woman held up a long wooden spoon. Her other hand held a baggie of ice. It wasn't much, but it was the best she could do right now.

"Perfect." Hazel took it from her hands and showed it to Ebba. "I am going to stabilize your wrist, Ebba. That means I am going to tie it to this spoon."

"With what?" Tears ran down her cheeks, but she looked confused. Children, even those in pain, were often full of questions. It was one of the things she loved about specializing in pediatrics.

"With this." Hazel undid the ribbon she'd tied her ponytail with this morning. It was soft, and a pretty pink.

As soon as she undid the bow, her hair popped out, wet curls falling everywhere.

Ebba laughed, a small sound, but a good one.

"My hair gets a little curly when it's wet." Hazel winked as she carefully lifted Ebba's wrist.

"A little?" One always heard the truth from the youngest.

Hazel wrapped the wrist then pulled Ebba's sleeve over the makeshift construct and put the ice on. Ebba sucked in a deep breath, then relaxed a little.

Ice would help with the swelling and numb a bit of the pain.

"As soon as we land, we're going to go to hospital for an X-ray."

"You're coming, too?"

"Of course." She hadn't really planned to. There wasn't a reason to. She didn't start until tomorrow; nothing like leaving it to the last minute to arrive.

This would let her get an idea of the hospital before starting.

And keep me from thinking about walking into a small furnished apartment on an island where the only person I know wears a crown and left me without so much as a real goodbye.

"A child crossing on the ferry this morning slipped and fell."

"Broken leg or wrist?" He hated that it didn't surprise him. There'd been far more accidents on the ferry lately. The island nation sat just below the Arctic Circle. Which meant even into the summer there was snow over much of the north, and down by the coast an icy drizzle fell.

The ferry dock was old, slippery and becoming more hazardous. He'd raise the issue with his brother later this week. Though he wasn't sure that it would do much good.

King Erik wasn't as focused on the aristocracy and their problems as his father...but he still didn't enjoy hearing Syver's "complaints."

In fact, he didn't enjoy hearing from Syver at all. His mother might raise the issue for him, but he doubted it. She rarely brought his concerns before the King.

If the crown didn't have interest in the issues, then Syver would use one of his other methods. Over the last several years, he'd become adept at maneuvering without the full approval of the crown.

If the captain didn't have the finances for the repairs, Syver would offer a small no interest loan out of the investment fund he'd set up. The one where he regularly turned down high-profile society projects his brother pitched.

His fund was for those without access to other money. The repairs benefited everyone, and the captain maintained the business his family had managed for at least four generations.

In his brother's five-year reign, Erik had reversed some of the damage his father's reign's focus on the aristocracy created. But he'd not gone far enough, in Syver's opinion.

There were beautiful buildings for the royal family, areas the average citizen never saw. But the price for their citizens had been steep. Resulting in a large-scale emigration.

He wasn't the only one banished from his home. He wanted as many of Fönn's residents to return as possible. And he could not understand why that made him even more of an outsider in his family.

It was easy to see their citizens struggled under aging infrastructure, bad tax codes and numerous other issues. Issues that didn't impact the insulated aristocracy. Issues many of the leading families of the island didn't care about.

Taking care of the country's health infrastructure was Syver's primary goal, which would be easier if his brother didn't constantly remind him that he wasn't really royal. Or keep him from leading the initiative.

But the imposter heir kept trying. With enough work, maybe he could make Erik and his mother accept that just because he didn't have King Eirvin's blood didn't mean he wasn't family.

"The good news is there was a nurse on board. She took command of the situation according to the notes the captain relayed." Meg, a recent travel nurse from Maine, turned Fönn resident when her contract ended, looked up from the tablet chart.

"That is good news." The words felt stilted, but Meg didn't seem to notice as she turned back to work.

Nurse...taking charge.

Hazel.

She started tomorrow and arrived today. Something the other employees didn't realize; something no one knew the Prince was tracking. He'd watched the manifests for his friend, worrying when her arrival date slipped closer without her name appearing on a flight or the ferry records.

Most of the travel staff they hired arrived at least a week early to get settled. But not Hazel.

He didn't know what to make of her late arrival. Her résumé said she could be available in a week's time. That she was looking to leave England. So why had she waited so long to arrive?

When Human Resources sent out the pack of résumés for new travel contracts two months ago, his mind had swirled at her name.

He'd picked up the phone immediately. The résumé pack was mostly so the doctors and head nurse knew what the pool looked like. Not to give hiring advice. He hadn't cared. He wanted Hazel here.

Now!

He'd mentioned that he'd worked with her at London Pediatric Hospital. That she was a wonderful nurse and would be an asset to the team. He'd left off that they'd been roommates.

Fönn's media had been consumed with King Eirvin's passing and Erik's rise to the throne when he'd arrived. No one had paid much attention to Syver's return. And Hazel had never given an interview about her relationship with him. Something his brother had worried over, but not Syver.

He and Hazel had been genuine friends. Leaving the way he had was still the biggest mistake he'd ever made. He should have put his foot down, stayed until she got home.

At the very least, he should have called immediately after he landed in Fönn. Invited her to join him, even. But the whirlwind of King Eirvin's funeral, comforting his mother, taking part in his brother's coronation and finally the investigation into the state of the country's health affairs had meshed together in a month of meetings, crisis talks and shakeups to ministry positions.

By the time he'd come up for air, thirty days had passed. Her mobile number suddenly didn't work, or she'd blocked him. He'd flown back to London, and found their flat empty.

The pain of standing in that empty set of rooms, of not being able to reach her. He'd thought of going to the hospital, but after living in the city for nearly a decade anonymously, this time, anonymity wasn't an option.

A diplomat arrived at the flat. And then the media. The life he'd had before…with Hazel…a distant memory. He'd flown out hours later, without ever finding her.

But she was coming here now. He could make it up to her. And maybe pick back up the friendship he'd cherished most in his life.

"Hi. I'm Hazel Simpson. I've got a seven-year-old female, Ebba."

"Broke her wrist on the ferry." Meg's voice carried over the conversation, but Syver felt each of the nerves in his body light at the sound he hadn't heard in so long.

"The captain called ahead. Dr. Bernhardt is ready for her."

"Syver?"

"At the ready. It's good to see you, Hazel." Syver stepped beside Meg, his body vibrating. She was here. Really here.

Her dark hair was curlier than he remembered, with water dripping from it.

Her hazel eyes held his for the briefest moment before dropping to the little one's level. "You are in expert hands, Ebba. It was so nice to meet you."

"You're not staying?"

"Hazel has a lot to do, honey. It was nice of her to come to hospital with us." Ebba's mum kissed the top of her daughter's head.

"But I have her ribbon."

Syver looked over the counter. A wooden spoon and pink ribbon stabilized the little girl's arm. The ribbon that had probably tied Hazel's curls.

"A wooden spoon?" He looked at her. "That is inventive, Hazel."

A look flashed in her eyes…a warning? It passed so quickly.

"Well, the ferry first aid kit was more than a

little lacking. Her wrist has had ice on it to reduce swelling. Bruising occurred immediately."

An orderly arrived. "Someone looking for an X-ray?"

Ebba's lip trembled. "Thank you, Hazel."

Hazel looked to the orderly, then to the child. She hesitated only a moment. "I'll see you when you get out, okay?" She smiled as Ebba's mother mouthed a thank you.

The little girl and her mum disappeared around the corner, and he saw Hazel's shoulders sag before straightening and looking at him. He waited for her to say something…anything, but no words fell from her full lips.

"That was nice of you," Meg murmured, breaking the awkward silence, as she looked from Hazel to Syver.

He could see the questions building behind Meg's eyes. It must be clear they knew each other. *She called me Syver.* No one did that. He was Dr. Bernhardt or Prince Syver. Never just Syver.

Not that it mattered. He had no intention of answering questions. Particularly before he talked to Hazel alone.

"Ebba's grandfather passed last week. They were returning home from his funeral. I guess he moved abroad in retirement." Hazel shrugged. "She's exhausted from travel, as is her mum, and sad."

"Big feelings." Syver made a note to give her mother a pamphlet on helping children with grief.

People often saw children as little adults, even though their brains weren't fully developed, and emotional regulation was something many adults struggled with.

"Yes. Combine that with a broken wrist—it's a lot." Hazel looked down the hall to where the orderly had taken Ebba and her mum. "Is there a phone I can use? I need to make sure no one delivers my stuff for another hour or two. Not that there is much of it."

Syver's heart ached at the hurt in that last phrase. Once he'd have known exactly why Hazel was hurt, or tired, or happy or anything. But right now, she didn't even hold eye contact with him.

If this reunion was taking place anywhere else, he'd ask—directly. But Meg had already caught a link between them. He wasn't ashamed of his time with Hazel, but she'd not wanted to stay in touch. He'd wanted to honor that.

So, he didn't talk about his time with her. Even his mother only knew that he'd had a roommate he'd treasured. And lost when he answered the call to come home with no notice.

Meg handed over the desk phone, but Syver jumped in. "I'll put in a call. Make sure everything is set up fine."

"Oh." Meg grinned and looked at Hazel. "That's perfect. Working with a doctor/prince has some benefits. His people will handle it perfectly."

His people. Such a weird statement. One that

after five years as the heir to the throne still felt uncomfortable. There were several limitations on Syver; things most people never saw. However, getting her stuff picked up and delivered, that was well within his abilities.

Hazel met his gaze then, her eyes finally holding his. His soul jumped. It was a ridiculous phrase; he knew that. Knew it wasn't even possible, but his inner self felt like it was coming home, finally.

He'd left London, lived in Fönn for years, but home. Home still felt elusive.

Because Hazel was missing.

"You don't have to, Syver… Dr. Bernhardt." Her voice was firm, but he saw her fingers twitch.

Looking at her hands, his chest caught. Each of her nail beds was red, picked over and over. He'd watched her pick her thumb when stressed, but for all of them to be so angry.

What happened?

He couldn't ask that here, but he could try to make her comfortable about using his name. "Syver works." He wanted her to use it. His colleagues referred to him as Dr. Bernhardt, and the people called him Prince Syver.

An upgrade from the barely controlled sneer previously attached to *Your Highness* people used when he first returned. A sign of respect, he knew, but he enjoyed hearing Syver. Just Syver…

Spoken in her sweet alto tone.

He swallowed, uncomfortable at the realization

of how much he wanted it. And the sensation that the want bordered up against a feeling that differed from the friendly bond they'd had for so long.

"Well…" Meg's voice was bright, a reminder that she was there.

Syver felt heat burn around the collar of his scrubs. "I'll place the call now, Hazel. I'll handle everything, promise."

There was that look again.

"Haz—"

"If you insist." She crossed her arms and looked at the floor.

"I do." He grinned, though it felt off. She was upset and trying to hide it. And he had no insight… deserved none.

"Why don't I give you a quick tour? You know, cut down on the things you need tomorrow for your first day." Meg stepped around the desk, her eyes meeting Syver's.

Yep, the nurse from Maine had questions…ones she'd ask Hazel and then come for him. Hazel could answer as she liked, but Syver would not break.

Their time together was too precious to be used as idle gossip.

"After I can show you to the room where Dr. Bernhardt will put on Ebba's cast."

"Sounds good." Hazel unzipped her coat, the oversize pink jumper she wore swallowing her slight frame. "I'll see you later, Dr. Bernhardt."

The two women headed off, and Syver leaned

against the counter. Hazel was here. She was really here.

And she'd called him Dr. Bernhardt. *Intentionally.*

How he hated that barrier. They'd never had one before. There were things he needed to say, things to apologize for. Better to do it fast.

He picked up the phone, arranged for Hazel's things to be unpacked and for a dinner delivery.

Today was a lot. After all, she'd left her home country, arrived in a new one, given aid to a wee one on the ferry, then come face-to-face with the roommate who'd abandoned her. An overwhelming twenty-four hours to be sure.

At least he could take care of her a little.

"Hazel!"

Shivers raced down her spine as Syver's voice hit her back. She'd stayed long enough to see Ebba's pretty pink cast. Hovering in the room and trying to keep her eyes from Syver. Now her goal of stealing out was failing before she'd set foot in the parking lot.

She was running from Syver, and the torrent of feelings his sight brought her.

After the cast was on, when saying goodbye, Ebba's mother had quietly whispered that everyone got used to Prince Syver just being among them. She'd kindly explained how being in royalty's presence was a little uncomfortable for everyone at first. But not to worry because he wasn't like most royals.

She knew that. After all, Hazel had lived with him. For two years.

Sort of.

Prince Syver was a mystery. A person she knew of from news and blog articles. The man she'd known was simply Syver. Her best friend.

Her best friend who'd abandoned her.

Left her to fend off all the questions. Not seen the shocked looks and heard the exasperated sighs when Hazel swore she hadn't known. That wasn't the worst, though.

No. It was the loneliness, the lack of his presence. The absence of the feelings she got when he was around. That was what she'd missed most.

It was that feeling that she'd chased with Alec. Pretending that with enough time, enough understanding, she could make those feelings happen again. Then her life had fallen apart.

That wasn't Syver's fault, but she'd wondered more than once what would have happened if he'd stayed.

Was that selfish? Maybe. But when she'd needed someone the most, the person she'd wanted to run to was gone.

And yet, I came here.

"Hazel!" The baritone sound of his voice now heated her blood. What was that? Remnants of the long day? Maybe. Whatever it was, it would disappear. It had to.

In less than sixteen hours, she was going to walk back through the hospital doors. She needed to get to her flat. Settle herself.

She truly hadn't expected to ever see him again. Maybe part of her had hoped, but working with him, she'd never let herself think of that. There were so many things she wanted to say. She wanted to confront him, tell him how his absence had affected every aspect of her life. How hurt she was.

Underneath that frustration was something else, too. The urge to run into his arms. To collapse into her once safe space. But Syver wasn't that—hadn't been that since he left.

It was clear they were going to be working together. Syver had always worked closely with the nurses, seeing them as part of the team. So she'd see him...a lot!

And as Meg's pointed questions about the looks he gave her reminded Hazel of their connection, the easy one they had, hints of it still simmered beneath the years and distance.

If it was that obvious, better to address it before they worked their first shift.

Turning, she bit her lip to keep the smile her brain wanted to form from appearing. She was lonely. It had been a rough year, a rough few years, and her soul wanted to jump into friendship. To recover something she'd thought lost forever.

But she wasn't the naive woman she'd been. Life had thrust so many choices upon her. From her mother's choices to Alec's, she'd let those choices wash over her rather than address conflict head-on.

The woman she'd been was gone. Hazel faced conflict now. Noticed the warning signs and addressed issues. Truth might hurt, but it was better than a fantasy.

Crossing her arms, she waited for him to reach her. Had he always been so tall…so handsome?

Yes.

It was something all her female colleagues, and a few of her male colleagues, had commented on. How did you live with such a beautiful man and not get turned on by him?

Because he'd been her friend. She'd loved him, but it hadn't felt romantic. Sure, her heart had calmed around him, and maybe she'd felt better in his presence than anyone else's, but that was the definition of their friendship.

Best friends. Two peas in a pod, who'd snuggled on the couch, laughed at silly and not-so-silly jokes. Made dinner and griped about work frustrations. Her other half who understood when she'd had a bad day. The one she'd leaned on.

Hazel had grown up jumping between small flats as her mother moved from one partner to another. Her mum always hoping the next guy was her knight in shining armor and blaming their abandonment on Hazel when things didn't work out.

The seminomadic life hadn't allowed for any deep childhood friendships to form. But it had felt like she and Syver had one.

Then he just left me.

"It was kind of you to come with Ebba and stay while I fitted her cast." Syver pushed his hands into his pockets. Was that still a tell for when he was nervous? "Is your ride on its way?"

She looked at the parking lot, her cheeks heating as she realized she had no ride. Rushing from the hospital as soon as they'd discharged Ebba, hoping to avoid this interaction, had gotten her here. And this was why she was supposed to address conflict head-on these days.

First day failure, because no taxi was coming to rescue her.

So step up now, Hazel.

"I don't have a ride. I guess that is something I should have thought about." She was glad the hood of the parka offered some cover for the heat coating her face. "Suppose I need to go back in and place a call."

"My shift's over. Why don't I take you to your flat?" He held up a hand. "Before you argue, I don't have to—I know. But let me anyway. I think we need to chat."

They did. This wasn't the case of some man disappearing and wondering why. She knew he'd ghosted her. He was a royal, and she was about as far from blue blood as possible. Still, there were things to say. Better to hash it out before they started working together.

She nodded, not quite trusting her voice.

"I need to change real quick. Don't move, okay?"

"I'm not the one who left with no warning, no ability to call, no forwarding address." The words were out, the years of hurt spilling uncontrolled into the open.

Syver flinched. Her words cut, and she hated that part of her was glad. She'd faced the media, the questions, the hate, alone. While he'd lived in a palace…because his father died. Her throat tightened.

"Hazel… I…"

Accepting confrontation when necessary was one thing, cruelty, another. She held up a hand. "Sorry. That was uncalled for." His family needed him; his country needed him. Hazel Simpson could not compare to those responsibilities.

"Hazel—"

"It's fine, Syver." She nodded to the hospital. "I'm tired and grouchy. Go get changed before I hire a taxi." It was an empty threat. She had no plans to leave, even if she could magic transportation to the parking lot.

He looked back at the hospital, then stepped close to her. Less than an arm's length separated them, and part of her brain screamed for her to move closer. Her heart remembered how safe she'd felt in his arms.

A safety she'd craved but hadn't felt since he left.

Her brain remembered other things, though. Recalled the sleepless nights, the tear-soaked pillows. So, her feet stayed planted.

"I'm not leaving you, ever again."

He raised his hand. For a moment she thought he'd cup her cheek, but then he pulled back.

"I promise, Hazel."

"Big promise." Hazel winked, trying to defuse some of the tension. They'd shared an easy banter once, a push and pull that looked almost scripted but came so naturally.

This wasn't five years ago, though. "And easy promise, when we're in your country." This was his place, where he was a prince. And she was just Hazel. Something that hadn't ever been enough.

"My country or not, it's true." Then he turned on his heel, nearly jogging through the hospital doors.

He returned in record time. So maybe he hadn't completely trusted her to stay put.

But it was the backpack on his shoulder that caught her eye. Navy blue, with patches…the bag she'd gotten him for his birthday.

The bag she'd found in a secondhand store. Vintage patches covering it. She'd purchased it immediately. Then unknowingly given it to a prince. "You still have that?"

Syver patted the strap. "Of course. Best gift I've ever gotten."

"I doubt that." Hazel murmured as she followed

him to a car parked in a slot for Dr. Bernhardt. Designated parking…a nice perk.

She slid into the leather seats, surprised when he started the car, but didn't pull out of the parking spot.

"Hazel." His voice was soft, the same voice she'd heard in so many dreams since he'd left. "I need you to know something."

She turned, her brain bouncing between excitement that she was finally with her friend again, uncertainty that she was finally with her friend again, anger and a fourth emotion pooling in her body that for a second felt like desire.

"I enjoyed every single minute of our friendship. It was the best time of my life." Drumming against the steering wheel, he looked at the car's ceiling, then back at her. "I never expected to come home to find Security in the flat…"

His voice died away, but there was a look in his eyes. Uncertainty or longing, or something else entirely? She wasn't sure.

He took a deep breath, reaching for her hand, but pulling back before he actually connected.

She ached to close the connection. But too much time and distance hovered in those few inches.

"But?" She looked away as she asked the question. Her life seemed like a never-ending series of *but*s.

I'd take you with me, but… insert random man

Mum was dating ...*doesn't like children. So Nan will look after you for a while.*

I'd take you on vacation, but it's just the boys.

I believe you didn't know about Alec's crimes, but the rest of the staff have doubts. You can't be effective if no one trusts you.

"But…" he waited, and she finally turned to look at him. "I should have told you who I was. It was selfish. I didn't think of myself as a prince. King Eirvin…well, let's just say he didn't miss me while I was gone."

Do all royals refer to their parents by their titles? It felt off. A hint of anger…and acceptance.

Unfortunately, a parent not missing you, she understood. She hated that he'd experienced it, too.

"I just want you to know that if I could do it over, I'd change several things in my life, but never the time I spent with you as my friend."

Friend. Why did that word leave a hole in her chest? They'd been friends. It was the right description—so why did she wish he'd embellished it?

All of his words spoke of the past. A friendship that had served him for the time. And now…and now they were colleagues. Just colleagues.

"Thank you, Syver."

He took a deep breath, looked at her, then turned his head and pulled out of the parking lot. Silence settled around them. It wasn't nearly as comfortable as the silences they'd enjoyed as roommates. Quiet times when they were lost in their own thoughts.

But it didn't bother her either. Silence from Alec had been a sign of trouble. A warning that his day had gone off and he might take that frustration out on her.

He'd never hit her, but as her counselor pointed out, abuse came in many forms. He'd honed his blade by leveraging her childhood trauma against her. If her mother didn't want her, why would anyone else? He'd helped her get her job. Without him, she was nothing.

They were just words, but they'd cut millions of slices into her soul.

Syver parked the car in front of a row of flats, pointing at the one on the end. "Palace staff delivered your bags a few hours ago. I asked them to stock the pantries and takeaway is in the fridge, too. Enough for you to have leftovers."

Enough to invite you in.

But she would not do that. She needed to process today. Decompress and settle in. Still. It was the nicest thing anyone had done for her in…well, the nicest thing done for her since Syver left.

"Thank you. Again." Hazel sighed as she crossed off some of the many items on her mental to-do list. "Do you help each of the traveling nurses?"

She'd meant the question to sound lighter than it had come out. However, like all words, once delivered, there was no way to recall them.

"No. But I've been excited since I rushed your résumé to the HR department."

Rushed my résumé...

The hiring official hadn't mentioned that. If he'd recommended her, a prince, could they have chosen a different candidate? Was she here because of Syver?

There's always someone better. Her mother's voice echoed in her brain.

No, Hazel wasn't letting that toxic thought take residence. She was more than qualified, more than a decade in pediatrics and five years as an advanced nurse-practitioner, often called an ANP.

"I'm happy you're here." Syver's face was so open, carefree. Like when they'd lived together.

In the images she saw on blogs and in gossip rags, he was controlled, regal. She reached her hand across the console and squeezed his.

The connection lasted less than a second, but she already wanted a hug. Wanted to invite him upstairs and reconnect. Lay her problems at his feet and rest for a while.

But he was Prince Syver now, and she was still Hazel Simpson. A lifetime of difference hung between the last five years, and she wasn't sure how to cross it. Or if she should.

So she offered a smile instead. "I'm happy I'm here, too." Then she slid out of the car, not trusting herself to stay any longer.

CHAPTER TWO

"Questions?" Clara, Fönn Children's Hospital human resource manager, leaned across her desk.

She had one. Not about this morning's orientation or job expectations, but one that had hammered through her brain all night. Not asking meant continued worries. And her brain, once latched on to a thought, rarely released it.

However, asking brought its own issues. *Fear is something you learned to move past. Take control of your situation and hold on to yourself.*

As her counselor had reminded her, humans often thought the worst when the actual result was nowhere close to it.

"One. And it's off topic." Hazel's stomach clenched, but it was best to know if they'd hired her because Syver pushed for it. If she'd landed in a new place just to be chased by the same issues as before.

If once more, her proximity to a man with power had made a difference. The physician at the private clinic had wanted the opportunity to invest in Alec's business. Not her expertise.

Or not *only* her expertise.

"Dr. Bernhardt was kind enough to drive me home last night—"

"You call him Dr. Bernhardt?"

The knot in her stomach tightened as Clara raised a brow, confusion clear on her face. Had she expected her to use his royal title or to call him Syver—because of their connection? "Why wouldn't I?"

She'd rarely spoken of their time together. He was her colleague. Her colleagues in London knew she'd lived with a prince. But after the news ruckus died off, people largely forgot her connection to the royal family of Fönn.

She'd never given an interview, something she was proud of. There were times when she could've used the money. Though she doubted the tabloids really wanted it. Their story wasn't exactly exciting. There were no salacious details to reveal. Just friendly reminders of the man she'd known.

Clara's eyebrows pulled together, and the tips of her lips turned down just barely. "It's just—he indicated when he prioritized your hiring that he knew you personally. He was gone for a while."

Clara's eyes caught hers. The same look Hazel had seen in Meg's eyes yesterday. A curiosity… probably wondering how a nurse from Nowhere, England knew the heir to Fönn's throne by name.

She would not react. The knife turning in her soul would not get the upper hand. Even if Hazel wanted to slink away.

First day and she was here because of Syver.

Should I have seen this sign? Should I have questioned?

How would she have even done that?

And it wasn't the first time, either. That stung. Once more she hadn't really earned her place.

It was her mother's favorite line.

People give you things, Hazel. You never earn anything.

Her mother believed Hazel should be glad she'd kept her when her father left. Glad for the necessities she'd provided. Things Hazel hadn't earned… couldn't earn, no matter her grades or attempts to please.

When her grades came back with excellent marks, her mother insisted Hazel's success was only because of the pressure she'd put on her. *Pressure. Trauma*…apparently those words were interchangeable.

And then Alec used his connections to recommend her to the private clinic she'd worked at.

It didn't matter how hard she worked. There'd always been someone who'd questioned if she deserved what she'd achieved. And now a prince had prioritized her résumé.

If she displeased him, would the hospital drop her contract?

"So Syver… Dr. Bernhardt…is the reason you hired me?" The words tasted like ash as she forced them out. Better to know than guess was only true if it wasn't the worst-case scenario.

"You were a top candidate but." She shrugged. "I mean, knowing people is how the world works, right? So Prince Syver's recommendation didn't hurt. Was that your question?" Clara looked genuinely confused. Like it was silly to even worry about.

But if you'd had someone take your position because of your ex…

She'd signed a contract. She was in Fönn for a year. Syver's recommendation or not. "I told you it was off topic."

Hazel knew her smile was forced, but there was no good way to segue out of the topic she'd raised.

"You're a qualified ANP, and Fönn is still recovering from years of mass exodus. We're all pleased you accepted the position." Clara's beeper went off, and she looked at it. "I need to run, unless you need something else?"

"No, thank you. I'll find Meg for the next round of orientation." What was done was done. Clara was right. She was a qualified ANP, and people used connections all the time to land positions. That the only connection she had was a criminal con man made her different from most.

I've got Syver.

Her body warmed as his face danced in her mind. And not as just a friend. What was that? Even though it frustrated her knowing his recommendation had, at the very least, been a selling point for her hiring, all her mind wanted to consider was how handsome he'd been carrying the backpack she'd given him.

She'd thought more about him almost reaching for her hand than about replaying his words about the job. Her mind questioning what would have happened if she'd closed the distance.

Nothing. Nothing would have happened.

"Good day, Hazel. I think that puts me at five hundred and one."

Her body ached at the greeting. There were a few times over the years where she thought she'd heard him. It always put her in a sour mood when she reminded herself that the game was over.

She'd missed the game. But they were strangers now. Playing it felt off. "Good morning, Dr. Bernhardt." She didn't acknowledge the count. Didn't make a joke, even though she wanted to.

Colleagues. They were just colleagues.

"You okay?" He wore blue scrubs with a cartoon bird stenciled on the pocket. It screamed *pediatrics*, and the scrubs were tailored to fit his body perfectly.

Of course they are. He is a prince.

At her hospital, a few of the doctors had purchased and tailored their own scrubs. Hazel had always just gotten hers from the bin the hospital provided. Something she planned to do here, too.

But she could appreciate the fineness that was Syver.

Seriously! How did she pull those thoughts from her brain? After all, she'd just learned of his recommendation.

A recommendation most people want, Hazel!

Most people would be pleased. So why was she so determined to be put off by it?

Alec's action had imploded her career. But Syver was as different from her con man ex as possible. He was her friend. Or at least he had been.

And none of those mental ramblings explained why her thoughts kept rotating back to Syver's good looks.

"I'm fine. Dr. Bernhardt."

"Again. I prefer Syver." He winked and held his hand out, gesturing to a hallway. "Any interest in lunch?"

Yes.

"I'm supposed to find Meg. Go over a few things and then, if they need me, help with patients." Hazel pulled at the skin around her fingernails. A nervous habit that she'd never fully broken. One that had worsened after Alec's arrest. "Not hungry anyway."

Her stomach rumbled, and Syver raised an eyebrow as he dug his hands into his pockets. At least she wasn't the only one uncomfortable with the shift that time and distance had done to their relationship. "I don't like to use the term *liar*," Syver teased.

"But it's true." She smiled, unconsciously, then wiped it from her face. It would be so easy to flip back into the friendly scripts they'd used. To play the hello game, to pick back up the inside jokes that had made her days so happy.

To lean on him. Leaning on him was why his disappearance was so rough. Leaning on Alec was why she was here to begin with. Hazel couldn't let herself lean on anyone. Not again.

He pursed his lips and looked toward the stairwell that led to the lower floor. "I've got a bit of a break. So, I'm grabbing a sandwich."

He turned and started down the stairs. She knew he wouldn't ask again. Wasn't pushing. Just letting the offer stand. And that made her want to follow even more.

Still, she hesitated. Then her stomach rumbled again. She had half a shift left, and medical staff learned to take breaks when the opportunities presented themselves.

It was only when she was standing in line behind him that she wondered what people would think of the two of them eating together. Staff ate together regularly, but she was new, he was the Prince.

And he recommended my résumé.

Things she should've considered before following him.

Sliding across the table from him, she wondered how fast she could gobble the hummus-and-tomato sandwich without seeming rude.

"I'm not pushing, Hazel, but your fingernails look worse than I've ever seen." Syver glanced at her hands, then picked up his sandwich. "Are you all right?"

The urge to lay everything out. To tell him why she was here. To joke that her fingers had looked nearly normal before Alec's arrest. But then she'd have to admit that her boyfriend had been arrested.

And that she'd lived with a man who'd treated her poorly and she'd accepted it. That still stung.

It was a hard lesson, but she'd sworn she wasn't going to accept less again. That no one would question her place in the world again. If someone couldn't accept her as she was, then they didn't get her at all.

She'd applied to be an international travel nurse and planned to start anew.

Then I came to the one other place in the world that I knew someone—how daring.

"It's been a long a year, or a long few years, I guess. I came to Fönn to start over." Her hand slid across the table toward his. His fingers flexed just before she pulled back.

She wanted to cross her arms, keep herself rooted in place so she wouldn't give in to the desire to reach for him. To touch him. That was the past and she needed to focus on the future.

On taking care of herself.

"I need to prove to myself I can do things on my own." She ran her finger over the broken skin of her thumb, the urge to rub it for a few seconds, or longer, hitting hard. But she refocused on her sandwich.

"I appreciate you forwarding my résumé." There, the words were out. She'd acknowledged the connection and his potential role. Address things head-on. That was the best route. The route she'd sworn she'd take now, no matter the consequences.

"I didn't forward your résumé." Syver took a big bite of his lunch and shrugged. "At least, not directly. I saw your résumé on the top of the packet and told Clara we needed to see if you'd come, but your résumé was always one of, if not the, top candidate for the position. I just put in a good word."

A good word…from a prince. Surely, he knew how much his words mattered?

"You're a prince."

"Eh…" He took another bite of his sandwich.

Could he really not see the difference it made? "Still, that was nice of you. I didn't expect it and—" The desire to say what had happened, confide in him, lean back into the safety, welled in her chest. It would be so easy.

Easy routes were the fastest to heartbreak. Her watch buzzed, and she finished the last bit of her lunch. She needed to leave.

"That's my sign to find Meg."

Syver nodded, though she thought he wanted to say more. But he let her go.

Syver saw Hazel walk into the room and knew a frown was forming on his lips. A childhood spent being told to keep his face devoid of any emotion other than polite excitement, a fake emotion, made him hyperaware of the position of his face. Another thing he'd let drift away while in London.

Something he hadn't wanted to return when Erik asked him back. Yet the happy family, the acceptance he'd hoped for…hadn't appeared. It was sad that the ability to hide his thoughts had reappeared almost as soon as he landed.

A necessity for survival in the unfeeling palace.

Hazel's words at lunch ricocheted through his mind. Even if he hadn't put a word in for her, he couldn't imagine Clara not offering her a contract.

People use inside connections all the time.

That thought irked him. It was true and one of the many things he had fought against since his brother ascended the throne. The issue he and the King argued about most often. The aristocracy thrived on inside connections. It was how their world worked.

And the system was decidedly unfair for anyone not privy to the behind-closed-doors conversations.

But Hazel was the opposite of aristocracy. She'd gotten into a preparatory school because of good grades and used scholarships to cover the high cost.

Other than that, he knew little about her background. When her roommate situation had shifted suddenly because of an elopement, she'd said she couldn't rely on family. They'd grown up in different classes, but Syver understood that. He'd offered his place as a short-term retreat, only to love having a roommate.

Well, he'd love having Hazel as a roommate.

In the two years they'd lived together, they'd spent holidays together—working—so others could spend time with family. Despite the distance, his mother always sent birthday and holiday gifts.

Small items, items that let him cling to the idea that at least one person in Fönn still thought of him.

The only gifts Hazel received were from him.

If Clara hadn't wanted to hire Hazel…well, if Clara hadn't thought she was an excellent candidate, Syver would have gone to bat for her.

Syver needed her here. Seeing her name had healed a deep wound. He'd have fought for her. Period.

But he hadn't had to, because Hazel's résumé spoke for itself.

"Fourteen-year-old girl exhibiting stomach cramps and fainting in Room Three." Hazel handed him the tablet chart. Her eyes shifted, and he could see words stuck there.

A concern, an uncertainty. Because she was new…or was it something else? "What is it?"

"I'm not offering a diagnosis—"

"I trust my nurses, but you're an ANP so you diagnose patients, too." They'd each worked with physicians who didn't trust other attending physicians or nurses. Those doctors had taught him exactly who he didn't want to be.

"I understand. I also don't want to add thoughts to your mind before you form your own opinion." Hazel shifted, then crossed her arms. "GI issues and fainting can indicate multiple diagnoses."

That was a good reason not to say something. Even if someone watched for it, unconscious bias affected all humans.

"But listen to her mother and watch the way she looks when her daughter talks about her symptoms."

Syver raised an eyebrow then nodded.

"I could be reading into things—"

"I doubt it." Syver looked over the tablet chart. The fourteen-year-old, Ida, complained about stomach cramps and had fainted during her gymnastic meet. "Let's go."

Stepping into the room, he offered Ida a smile. "Ida, I'm—"

"Prince Syver." She smiled as she looked up. Ida was hugging her knees and covered in a blanket.

"She was cold." Hazel answered his unspoken question. So their ability to read each other perfectly in work situations hadn't faded. That was going to come in handy.

Unfortunately, it didn't appear intact outside the hospital. They were stilted. Words clogged his throat, things that needed to be said, but he couldn't push out.

Still, she was here.

"My stomach is better now after the cracker Hazel gave me. It was just a long meet." She sighed and shifted, the blanket slipping off her shoulders.

Her collarbone stood out in the bright lights. He looked to Hazel and saw her attention focused on the same point.

Ida ran a hand over her arm. "Your arm hurt?"

"Oh." She pulled the blanket over her arm. "My skin's dry. It happens."

Anorexia nervosa. The diagnosis he knew Hazel feared. Disordered eating was a complicated diagnosis; it would be easier to treat a GI issue. Dry skin, the thin arms and being cold, he ticked them off mentally. All symptoms related to the body not getting enough nutrition.

There was no quick fix for body dysmorphia.

"Cracker?" Hazel started to cross her arms, and he watched her adjust her stance. Confrontation wouldn't work, but he understood the urge. It was easy to argue that you just needed to eat more. But Ida wouldn't respond to that. "I gave you two packets, eight crackers in each...did you eat more than one?"

Ida's eyes shifted to her mum, who held up the packets. "She handed them to me after the first one. I told you, you should have more." Her eyes shifted to Hazel, pain radiating through her features.

So Mum knew what the issue was too, and either had confided in Hazel or saw a partner in getting her daughter help.

Syver used the tablet chart to alert the nutritionist that they needed a consult. It was possible Ida had a GI bug, but if she did, it was a secondary diagnosis. The cramps were probably hunger pains and the fainting due to a lack of nutrients.

"You need to eat more than a few crackers, Ida. This is just to help with your hunger pains." He kept his tone light as he made another note for the nutritionist.

"I have a big competition next weekend." Ida's bottom lip wavered. "I'm already bigger than all the other girls. I can't even add half a pound."

She needed to add at least fifteen, ideally twenty-five. There was no way Ida was the largest gymnast, which was not a terrible thing. But with body dysmorphia it was likely Ida saw herself that way. And explaining that she wasn't wouldn't work.

That didn't keep her mother from trying. "You aren't. And even if you were, it wouldn't matter." Her mother's voice quivered. "And you need food for fuel, honey."

"I *need* to get extra rotations." Ida lifted her chin. "And to do that, I need to be as small as possible. Coach says so. If I want to compete at the next level, I have to sacrifice."

"Coach…" Her mother closed her mouth and hugged herself. "I want you healthy, Ida."

There was little Syver could do here other than refer Ida to Inpatient Services. Which he planned to do. But with disordered eating, the patient needed to see the problem.

That was one of the first steps on the long road to health. And having an adult in her life pushing for her to reach a next level—to lose weight—was not helpful. He wasn't sure what he could do about a coach encouraging disordered eating, but he'd figure that out after this consultation.

"Is next week the last meet?" Syver thought in-patient treatment needed to start immediately, but if next week was the last meet, holding off a few days might make it more likely that Ida would enter the program willingly. The odds of success went up drastically in those cases.

"There is no last meet." Her mother frowned and pushed a tear off her cheek. "We've been at the gym nearly every day since she turned seven."

"I have a gift—Coach says so." Ida curled tighter into the blanket. "A gift. I just have to sacrifice a little more."

"Ida." Hazel stepped forward, then sat on the side of the bed with her. "Does your hair fall out when you brush it?" Her voice was soft, but there was a tone of authority in it. Syver took a step back and looked to Ida's mum. If Hazel made a connection here, it would help them immensely.

"Everyone's does…" She brushed a tear off her cheek. "But yes."

"That's because the nutrients you get from food keep your scalp healthy and make your hair grow. And your skin itches?"

"No lotion Mum finds works. I've tried… I don't know, it feels like hundreds of kinds." Her voice was soft, tears coating each word.

"That's because the lack of nutrients is drying out your skin. It's also why you are so cold. As you lose muscle mass, your body can't regulate your temperature." Hazel took a deep breath, looked at Ida's mum and then continued, "And you're hungry all the time, right?"

Ida sucked in a breath, "If I were stronger, I wouldn't be."

Ida's mum put a hand over her mouth, and Syver saw tears trickle behind them, but she didn't make a noise. This was going to be a long road with many hills and valleys.

"No. You are so strong." Hazel held out her hand and Ida put her hand in hers. The bones of Ida's wrist so prevalent, Syver was shocked she wasn't breaking bones.

That was coming, though, if she didn't get help.

"Coach…" Ida bit back whatever she planned to say. "I'm tired, too." She leaned her head on her knees but didn't pull away from Hazel.

"Of course you are. Your body is a wonderful machine, but it needs nutrients. You are perfect, just the way you are. You don't owe anyone but yourself your best, sweetie."

"I don't want to give up, but… I think I need help, too. I'm torn, Mama. What do I do?" Ida started sobbing then and Hazel slid off the bed, shifting places with her mum who wrapped her arms around her daughter, sobs echoing between them.

Syver waited a few minutes, let the emotions of the room calm a bit, then started; "I've requested our nutritionist for a consult, and I will make a recommendation for inpatient treatment for disordered eating. As an emergency doctor, I can only do the referral, but if you have questions, call the desk here, ask for me. If I don't know, I will find someone who does."

Ida's mum mouthed *thank you* as he and Hazel walked out of the room. All of this information would be on the discharge paperwork, because he doubted her mother would remember, but that was okay.

Closing the door, Syver turned to Hazel. "That was impressive."

"A tiny baby step on the very long road that Ida is going to walk. Probably for the rest of her life." Hazel clenched her fists. "And her coach…"

"I'll have a look at that." Ida's statement worried him. Young adults were impressionable, but no sport was worth creating lifelong health problems.

Hazel let out a breath, her shoulders relaxing as she looked at him. "Working with a prince has perks, I guess."

"Occasionally." His family didn't give him much responsibility. The King rarely listened to him. The people liked him and that gave him some sway. Still, his suggestions were just that. Suggestions one could ignore.

"But you were the actual hero in there. Sitting with her, walking her through her symptoms, brilliant. Letting her acknowledge each one."

"A trick I saw a nutritionist use at the last clinic I worked at in London. Not my idea." Her eyes darted away from him, and she rocked back on her heels.

Hazel was getting ready to bolt. The uneasiness was already settling around them.

"It wasn't a trick, Hazel. It was skill, and the reason you are here." Before she could interrupt, he continued, "You told Ida she was perfect just the way she was. That she didn't owe anyone but herself her best."

He stepped closer and almost regretted it as the pull he'd noticed between them since she'd showed up yanked at him. Syver wasn't sure exactly what that was. But he pushed the feeling away as he held her bright eyes. This moment was about Hazel, not his own wants. Whatever those were.

"You can see it in others, so perfectly...why not yourself?" He smiled and stepped back.

Why does stepping away feel like I'm wading through sand?

It should be easy. They'd worked together for years as friends. Joked and had deep conversations on the bad days, but he hadn't felt drawn to her like this.

Had he?

Maybe he was just excited to have his friend back...

"Thank you, Dr. Bernhardt." She patted his arms, friction bolting through his body. Her eyes followed her hands and she yanked them back. Clearly, she hadn't meant to touch him. Hazel opened her mouth, then shifted and started down the hall.

In another lifetime he'd have made a clever joke, walked with her. Joked with her. Now he watched her go, wishing they weren't at work, wishing he could follow her.

CHAPTER THREE

"THANK YOU SO MUCH for agreeing to switch shifts!" Meg was nearly bouncing as she handed the tablet chart over. "Summer Nights is one of my favorite holidays, and I'm not even from Fönn."

And it didn't hurt that her boyfriend had indicated that he might propose this evening. Hazel didn't mention that, though. Meg was already nervous that she'd misread the signs.

The historian she was seeing was full of interesting tidbits and Meg was nearly certain he'd been bread-crumbing hints all week. But now that the night had arrived, the nerves set in.

She understood. How many signs had she misread over her lifetime? That was a list she had no desire to make.

"I hope you have fun."

"Oh, I will. Part of me feels bad that you'll miss the festival's opening. It's your first Summer Nights. At least it should be sl—" Meg clammed up, not wanting to jinx the staff by saying the night should be slow.

Hazel appreciated the concern, but holidays spent in the hospital were something she was very used to. Others had families to spend this time with.

Alone was how Hazel had grown up. Alone was how she'd spent so much time. And not wanting to be alone anymore was how she'd nearly gotten trapped with Alec. That wasn't a pretty realization, but one didn't address internal issues without acknowledging how trauma affected them.

"Don't worry about me." She winked. "The doctor and I will do fine." If the night really was slow, then she'd work through the stack of paperwork that always seemed to pile up, no matter how the staff endeavored to keep it under control.

"Dr. Bernhardt and you will be fine." Meg held up a hand and walked out.

"Syver?" His name slipped out. She still wasn't used to calling him Dr. Bernhardt, no matter how much she tried to remind herself.

"You called?"

Hazel spun and couldn't stop her smile as he leaned against the nurses' station. She wiped it off quickly. Since her first day, they'd worked a few shifts together.

Professionally—professionally they worked better than ever. Syver was now a full physician and so sure of himself. And she was an ANP. In the years they'd worked together, she was still getting her footing as a nurse, and he'd left right after finishing his residency. There'd still been a hint of professional uncertainty when they worked together last time.

The uncertainty was still there, but they were used to it. One didn't practice medicine without worrying that they were making the wrong choice or second-guessing tough choices.

At least good medical professionals didn't. Once you accepted that feeling, it made you a better professional.

Life had thrown them back together, and their ability to pick up on the needs of the patient and relay them to each other with minimal words, or sometimes even a look, was back.

Personally, though. Personally things felt stilted… and heated. It was such a weird combination.

She might be able to overlook it, if there wasn't an undercurrent in her blood every time she saw him.

Desire?

She woke with thoughts of him. Fell asleep thinking of him. Things that hadn't been there before, or maybe they had? History blurred with feelings she wasn't sure were actually there.

They'd been friends. No undercurrents of need or heat or whatever…except she wasn't so sure of that now.

He leaned toward her, and her body ached to close the distance. Something she'd done years ago without even thinking. They'd touched, friendly… light caresses. Things she'd missed so much when he was gone.

But now…now there were so many layers involved. Once, she might have thought he wanted to renew their friendship. Maybe he did. But she'd misread so many things. So, she kept her distance.

"Why aren't you at the festival?" She wasn't

from Fönn, and in London they'd worked all the
holidays together, but here he had family. And royal
responsibilities. The royal family opened the festival. She knew that; she read up on the festival—
on him. Though now that she'd blurted it out, she
realized he was never mentioned as attending the
opening night. The King and Queen featured prom-
inently on the flyers, but the flyer listed the Dowager Queen, too.

The articles mentioned he always attended the
closing night, but she'd assumed he was there other
days too.

After all, Syver was the heir to the throne.

"Looking to get rid of me, Hazel?"

She knew the words were a joke, but there was
something in his look. Sadness? Uncertainty.

Not really. Though it would be easier to be paired
with anyone else tonight. But she couldn't say that.

"Of course not." She reached for his arm again
but pulled back. Yep, that was too much of a reaction.

She couldn't pretend it upset her that he was here.
She enjoyed working with the other physicians in
the small pediatric hospital, but working with Syver
was her favorite.

Still, reaching for him, touching him *and* the heat
in her cheeks were too much for a work friendship.

We did it before.

"I just figured as Prince Syver you'd be at the

festival. Your family opens the festival, after all. A fancy opening ceremony, from what I read."

His eyebrows shifted on the word *family*, a deep crease appearing between his eyebrows for a second before vanishing. "Technically, the King opens the festival tonight. The Queen and Dowager Queen attend too, but my presence isn't necessary." There was a heaviness to the words. An acceptance coated with…coated with something, but she wasn't sure what.

"The last night is my favorite." He was still smiling, but she could hear the heaviness.

"Syver—"

"If you're free, come."

Free to come? Did he want her to, or was it just a slip? Ugh. Just ask!

"Do you want me to come?" It was only after the question was out that she realized he said she should come if she was free, not come with me.

Syver was probably just being nice. How did someone talk about attending a festival without asking the roommate you'd lived with for two years to come along? At least how did a person do it without seeming rude? She held her breath. Waiting for the no. Or the *I'll be sure to wave, if I see you* comment.

She ran a finger over her thumb, the urge to pick at the skin pulling at her, but she was getting better. Her week in Fönn had already calmed her nerves considerably. Not having colleagues cut you out of conversations or finding yourself walking in on gossip that went silent when you rounded the corner would lift anyone's spirit.

Now the only time she was nervous was when she was alone with Syver. Those were different nerves, though. Whether she wanted to admit it, she had a little crush on her former best friend.

Except he wasn't just Syver now. Hazel was crushing on the Prince of Fönn. The heir to the throne.

He'd always been handsome, but now…now she noticed more. Thought of him more. Ached to touch him, and not in the friendly way they'd always shared. The little touches, hugs, things she'd done without thinking before.

Fantasy was all right, as long as she remembered Syver would marry one of the country's aristocratic women. That was the custom The expectation for the heir to the throne. Something she knew because she'd kept up with him.

"I'll pick you up." Syver smiled, and the air around them popped.

Was that a good idea? Maybe not. Perhaps spending time with him outside the hospital would squash the feelings running too free in her soul.

"So what is the first night of the festival like here?" She asked, trying to force her brain away from the idea of hugging Syver and raising her head and kissing…

He cleared his throat; at least she wasn't the only one uncomfortable here.

"Well, there is a lantern ceremony. The King lights the first one, then the rest of the festivalgoers follow suit. The entire sky looks like floating stars. As a kid I stood on the platform with my mother, brother and the King and just stared into the sky."

She'd meant what was the unit like tonight. The halls of the emergency department were quiet. It was a little unsettling. She and Syver were here, along with a handful of other nurses. And two floater doctors, one from the cardiac unit and one from neurology, were on call on their floors in case Syver needed aid.

It was something she'd not experienced in London. The emergency department had had a constant stream of small patients. Even the clinic she'd worked at after Alec's recommendation was busy from the moment it was open until at least an hour after the last patient walked out. She wasn't used to having any downtime, but life on Fönn was slower.

It was easier to breathe here. Like the weight she'd worn since birth was finally gone.

Like she was home. *Home.* Hazel didn't really have that. And a flat with rented furniture did not a home make. Still, Fönn was a good landing place after the chaos of Alec's arrest.

"Why do you always call your father the King?" The question landed like lead. Syver stood, and she saw the shift in his stance. It happened anytime someone brought his father up. She'd noticed it before, but in the quiet hallways it was suddenly on bright display.

Her hand twitched as she reached for him, then she put her hands in her pockets. They were alone, mostly, but this was still work. And there was still a barrier between them. The chasm of distance.

She could see the heaviness in his soul. His own weight—one she was sure wasn't there when they'd lived together.

Before he could dash away, a car pulled up. It slowed, and a teenager got out, then it drove off.

The teen walked in, his arm wrapped in a towel…soaked with blood.

"What happened?" Syver was moving around the call desk as Hazel followed suit.

"I fell on my way to the festival." The teen took a deep breath and slowly pulled the towel from his arm, displaying dozens of thorns. "Into my dad's prickly wild rosebush."

Unfortunately, the towel had likely pushed several of the thorns farther into the teen's skin and the grimace on his face hurt Hazel's heart. It wasn't a life-threatening emergency, but seeing a child, and teens were still children, in pain was the worst part of this job.

"Is your dad on his way in?" She'd seen a few parents drop their older kids right at the door, then find a parking spot before rushing back to their side.

"Um—" The teen looked to the door, then to

his feet. "He probably went to the festival. Technically, he's my stepdad. Though I don't remember a time…" He blew out a breath and shook his head. "I'm seventeen, so I can handle this."

The grimace reappeared, but he straightened his shoulders. He was trying to maintain his control, something a child shouldn't have to do, particularly when they were in pain.

Age didn't matter when you were hurt. She'd known from her earliest days that her mother didn't want her. Yet on her darkest days, Hazel had still wished for the comfort a mother might give.

She suspected the pain of knowing his stepfather wasn't coming back hurt as much as the dozens of tiny cuts on his arm. Hazel and Syver could patch those wounds…the others were not so easily healed.

"Of course you can." Syver nodded, but she could see the fury in his eyes. Yes, the young man could handle this, but he shouldn't have to. "Follow me."

The young man stepped beside Syver as they headed for the first room.

"I'm going to get some warm water," Hazel called. "I had a friend who fell in a rosebush. Long story, but it will help with the removal."

She dashed away and was back in a few minutes, carefully carting the water bath with Epsom salt. "It takes about ten minutes, then the removal won't hurt as much."

The teen put his arm in the water and immediately relaxed.

"Does it feel good?" Syver was pulling sterile tweezers from the room's storage supplies and materials for stitches.

"Yeah. Weird."

Hazel nodded, "It is. I lived next door to Annie when we were both around five. Her gran had a bunch of rosebushes in the center of her backyard. Beautiful. Late one night, we were playing tag and forgot where they were. Annie was tangled in the bushes for…well, it seemed like an eternity.

"After her gran got her out, she dropped her into an Epsom bath, then spent the night pulling thorns out." She looked at her watch, almost ten minutes gone. Fortunately for Annie, she'd fallen into a regular rosebush. Which, while painful, it didn't have the same number of thorns as the wild kind.

"We are lucky Hazel had such an experience, though her friend wasn't as lucky." Syver glanced at her, and she could see pain in his eyes, then it vanished.

She tried to read the issue, something they did so well in these situations, but nothing came to her. Whatever the problem, she didn't think it had to do with Carr's physical injury.

"That's ten minutes, Dr. Bernhardt. How do you want to rest his arm for the procedure?" There were thorns in Carr's hand, his elbow, everywhere. There was no position that wouldn't cause him at least a little pain.

"I wish my mum was here." Carr leaned his head back and blew out a breath.

Hazel looked to Syver. Asking to call her wasn't a great idea if she'd passed, but if she was available via phone, Hazel didn't mind asking.

"She's traveling. On a plane over the Atlantic, right now." Syver blew out a breath and looked at Carr's hand.

So that option was out. All right, she and Syver would do what they could to help the teen, but he'd always remember his stepfather's actions.

That damage could last a lifetime.

"Think you can hold up your arm long enough for me to get the thorns out of your hand, then you can rest on your hand while I work my way up the rest of your arm?"

"I can do that." Carr held up his hand. "Let's do this."

"That's the last one." Syver stitched up the last of Carr's wounds. The boy had held strong through the nearly hundred thorns he'd pulled from his skin and the thirty stitches in twenty cuts that wouldn't close on their own. His arm was a patchwork of cuts, but he'd done perfectly.

Carr's eyes were closed, his uninjured arm thrown over his eyes. The procedure had taken close to three hours. Luckily, Dr. Olsen had handled the other three cases that had wandered through the door. All minor injuries from the festival and quickly dispatched.

The teen was exhausted and sad.

Syver understood. He only knew his biological father was his mother's lover. He didn't know the man's name, only that she'd refused his offer to run away together. Probably because it would have meant leaving Erik.

The real royal. Syver was raised in the palace as a prince. King Eirvin had instructed everyone that they were to act as though Syver belonged.

He was part of the royal household, but acutely aware that he wasn't the same as Erik. He'd never felt loved by the King, and his mother only showed him affection when King Eirvin wasn't around. No matter what he accomplished, what he achieved, it wasn't enough.

He wasn't enough.

It wasn't until he was a teen that he'd understood why he was different, and that nothing he could do would change that.

"Your mobile is ringing. Caller ID says Mum." Hazel held up the phone. "Do you want me to talk to her or are you ready?"

Carr moved slowly, exhaustion coating his expression. "Can you tell her what's happening, then pass me the phone? I just… I don't want to."

"Of course." Hazel offered a comforting smile and sat on the edge of the bed as she answered.

"Hello, this is Hazel at the Fönn Children's Hospital. Carr is fine."

Syver heard the breath Carr's mum let out. It was the perfect way to answer the phone. Put the woman at ease—it was a skill Hazel had exuded in London and one he'd seen repeatedly in the last week.

She was excellent at her job, but it was deeper than that. She was meant to be a nurse. Meant to help people, to make them feel at ease. It was a trick one could learn, but you'd never be great at it, if it wasn't natural.

Hazel went over the basics of the injury and treatment. And Syver could tell from the answers that she'd talked to her husband first. And that the woman was furious her son was alone at the emergency department.

That was good. It meant Carr had a support system at home.

Something Syver didn't have. His mother loved him. But duty to the crown came before everything else. She'd wavered once, and had Syver, but since then she was the personification of duty.

His brother treated his wife, Queen Signe, better than King Eirvin had treated his queen. But it was still a marriage of convenience. A union meant to secure the royal line.

If Syver married, theirs was the type of marriage expected of him. A marriage of convenience where the bride knew the expectation was duty, not love.

His mother had attempted to set him up with a

few "appropriate" candidates. *If* a marriage was ever granted for him, it would be one like Erik and Signe's. Syver had given in to so many family expectations. Done so much for them.

But he'd refused that one. Better to remain single than fall into a union like his parents.

"Your mum wants to talk to you." Hazel handed the phone over. "Dr. Bernhardt and I are done. Do you want privacy, or would you like me to stay?"

"Stay, please." Carr picked up the phone, as Syver nodded to Hazel and stepped from the room.

He needed a few minutes to collect himself. Children hurting was the hardest part of this job. He could fix the cuts the rosebush dealt, but the injury his stepfather inflicted…

It was so close to thousands of wounds King Eirvan had laid on him. Wounds that scabbed but never fully healed.

Syver leaned against the wall, closing his eyes.

"I need to find my stepson. Now."

The voice was angry, and Syver opened his eyes. *Let me guess. Your wife called.*

It was the first line that came to his mind. The first line of the dress down he wanted to give. But that wasn't professional, and his son still had to live with him. At least until his mum got home. Patient safety had to come first.

"Carr had over a hundred thorns in his hand and arm. He needed thirty stitches. Not all in the same place, instead they had to be placed in the larger cuts with two or three stitches. Your *son* did fantastic."

The man's cheeks were red, and Syver could see the motions of trying to figure out how he was supposed to respond. "If he'd been listening to me, he wouldn't have fallen in the bushes to begin with."

That might be true. It might not be. It didn't matter. Carr had needed him here, and he wasn't.

"My nurse explained to his mum what happened and the treatment."

His eyes shifted to the left, and he clenched his fists before releasing them. "The first night of the festival is huge for my business."

"Yet you left early?" Syver raised a brow. The lantern lighting wouldn't happen until two hours after sunset. Which in summer meant almost midnight.

So he'd been able to step away now.

"My wife wanted me to check on Carr." He stuffed his hands in his pockets. "I wanted to talk to him before she called, but I guess…" He blew out a breath and some of the tightness in his body language relaxed, too.

He'd wanted to save face with his wife. But what of his son?

"Is Carr safe to go home with you?" It was an important question, one Syver needed answered correctly, and in a manner he believed.

"Yes." His stepfather kicked at the floor. "I won't pretend that tonight makes me look good." He ran a hand over his face. "But he's fine with me. I just never clicked with Carr like I did with his brothers."

"Because his brothers are biologically yours?"

The man pressed his lips together. And Syver didn't need confirmation. He'd lived this life; nothing he said would make much difference. It was sad, but this was a deep-seated issue the man in front of him needed to fix, if he was capable of it.

"Carr is a good kid. And you are missing out by not knowing him and loving him." Syver stuffed his hands in his pockets. "Room Three."

He stepped into the staff lounge, walked to the fridge and grabbed a bottle of water. He drank the whole thing down; his brain iced, but it was more comfortable than the thoughts racing through his head.

"Why does it matter whose blood runs through someone's veins?"

"It doesn't." Hazel's words were soft as she stepped to his side. "DNA doesn't make a family."

He'd not meant for anyone to hear the words. But he wasn't upset Hazel was here.

She went on, "Or at least DNA shouldn't. It also shouldn't matter that you get a girl when you want a boy. That was why my biological father left. Or rather, it's the reason my mum gave."

Her hand rested on his arm. It was comfort she was offering, comfort that should flow through him. But the touch felt like fire. Need, desire, the urge to pull her into his arms raced through him.

What is wrong with me?

They were at work. Carr's relationship with his stepfather mirrored his issues with King Eirvin. He'd spent the better part of the evening pulling thorns from a kid's arm. The last thing Syver should be thinking about was how Hazel touched.

Or how much he wanted to touch her.

"You okay?" Her words were coated with concern.

"Of course." He cleared the emotions from his throat, "It just hurts when a parent doesn't see their child as they should. And it's too common." That was the truth. Part of it.

He'd never spoken to anyone about his biological father. Technically, he wasn't allowed to. To hurt the crown meant hurting Fönn. And the royal family never hurt Fönn. At least not through scandal.

His father had banned the man's name from his mother's lips…something she'd followed even after his death. It was like they thought by not addressing it, Syver would be more of a true royal.

Yet, he was still the imposter heir, never quite good enough.

"Syver—"

"I'm fine, Hazel, and I don't want to discuss it any further."

She pulled her arm away, and he wanted to yank the words back. She'd offered him comfort. Despite the uncertainty still lying between them, she was coming to his aid, and he'd snapped at her.

He was a royal. An aristocrat, born with the silver spoon in his mouth. People figured he didn't have problems. Or if he did, they were easy enough to solve for a man in his position.

And most things could be. But not this.

"Hazel…"

"It's fine, Syver." She turned but paused at the door, then looked over her shoulder. "But if you ever want to discuss why *this* upset you so much, I'm still a pretty good listener."

A lifetime of holding on to this secret, the thing he was supposed to tell no one. The reason they'd forced him from Fönn.

He'd gotten a medical degree, but the palace could banish him again if he stepped out of line. And the children of Fönn deserved an advocate. One who wouldn't leave for better opportunities.

But knowing he was always a degree away from being cast out…how did he explain the lifetime of anger, hurt and frustration that left? He knew Hazel would understand, but letting that truth out, voicing the worries, made them real.

Strolling up to Hazel's door, Syver pulled on the collar of his jumper. It was a cool evening, but heat crept up his neck.

He'd expected her to call it off so many times this week. He'd waited for it, waiting to break from it. But she hadn't.

They were going to the final night of the Summer Festival. As…friends? The descriptor felt off.

This wasn't a date. Even if part of him wished it was. A tiny part, one he kept trying to ignore.

He was just glad his friend was back. The feelings rushing through him were an over-the-top reaction to seeing Hazel after so long. In a few more weeks, it would settle back down.

Is that what I want?

A lifetime of wondering what if?

Syver didn't want to travel that mental loop. Tonight was meant to be fun. A way to get back the friendship that he'd missed for so long. Tonight was simply two friends reconnecting.

Maybe this would clear the tension pulling through them. They still worked well together, better than he did with the rest of the staff, even after years away. But they were a bit off.

Even more since his outburst following Carr's procedure. He couldn't retract the harsh words, but he could show her the festival.

The first night of the festival was the biggest, and the crowds lightened as the week progressed. Tonight was the least attended event. But the last night of Summer Nights was one of his favorite things. He'd heard people calling the dimming of the lights sad.

That watching each section of the park go dark made them wish it wasn't over for the year.

For Syver, it was like a rebirth. Standing in the festival darkness with just the few who stayed all night, it was magical. Like starting anew.

And attending it with Hazel was a dream he'd never conjured come true.

She opened the door before he could raise his hand to knock. Her curly brown hair was pulled into a high ponytail, the curls spilling over her cheeks. Her lips were light pink, and so full. He caught himself staring at them and forced himself to look into her eyes instead.

If he'd hoped meeting her gaze would ease the clench in his chest, the butterflies in his stomach or the urge to lean toward her, he'd been sadly mistaken. The green hue called to him, his own special siren song.

"Ready?" His voice sounded hoarse as he stared at the woman he'd never been able to forget.

Hazel stepped out of the flat, her body brushing his for an instant, and Syver couldn't contain the sigh.

"Yes, I'm ready."

Yes. Yes.

He mentally screamed the word on repeat. He wanted to spend the last night of the festival with Hazel. Wanted to walk with her in the quiet, dimming streets. Wanted to see how she'd react to the night so few saw as a celebration.

"It surprised Meg you were going tonight." Hazel stepped next to him on the sidewalk. Her flat was less than a mile from the festival grounds and they'd agreed to walk. "I guess she didn't realize you always go on the last night. I joked that King Erik opens and Prince Syver closes."

Not technically.

He did always attend the closing, but he never pointed it out. "Who told you I always go to the closing?" Erik was part of the opening ceremonies. He lit the first candle. Syver attended the final night as a civilian. Or as much of a civilian as possible.

Many of the stalls closed once they'd sold out of their wares. It was quiet. Music ended an hour before the final light dimmed. It was almost meditative.

"Oh, I read it online on a…" Hazel's voice trailed off and then she let out a nervous laugh. "I…uh…" She ran a hand along her chin and then looked at him, her cheeks shading pink. Such a beautiful color. He wanted to run his finger over her cheek. He swallowed the thought.

Focus!

"Did you keep up with me on the tabloid blogs?" They focused on the royal family, and occasionally ran pieces on him. Usually when his brother fed a piece of gossip to push an uncomfortable story off him.

Syver wasn't sure what to make of the news that Hazel had kept track of him—sort of. In his mind, he'd figured she'd left their flat in London and rarely thought of him. If she'd followed him, what did that mean?

Syver wrapped an arm around her shoulder and

leaned his head against hers. It was an automatic reaction. One he'd done hundreds of times when they'd lived together.

But his body had never jolted, his nerves never fired, reminding him exactly which parts of his body connected with her. Maybe he should pull away, but that was the last thing he wanted, and Hazel sighed, a contented noise that raced right to his heart.

When he lifted his head, she rested hers against his shoulder as they kept moving. That cemented his choice. He'd hold her until she pulled back.

"Maybe." Another uncomfortable laugh followed. "I hated losing touch, and you weren't hard to find."

"If you hated losing touch, why did you block my mobile number?" The words were out before he could think them through. He'd tried...not fast enough, he admitted that, but listening to the dead air when he called, watching the text say undeliverable had broken his heart.

He didn't want to make her feel bad. He was the one who left; she got to react however she needed.

Hazel sighed as she stepped out of his arms. "I didn't."

"Hazel, I tried calling. I texted, I flew back to London, and you'd abandoned our flat. It hurt, but I also know leaving the way I did..."

"You came back?" Hazel stopped. Her mouth falling open as she shook her head. "For me?"

"For you." He pulled her to him then. Not the subtle around-the-shoulder hug they'd had. A full body, holding her as close to him as possible, hug.

His heart nearly exploding when she wrapped her arms around his waist. A piece of him snapped into place. The world felt like it tilted back to where it was supposed to be. Hazel with him. It just made sense—it always had.

When she stepped back, she took his hand, squeezing it. "You really came back for me?" She pursed her lips after repeating her words.

"I did. About a month after. Everything was so crazy when King Eirvin died, and then Erik ascended and the coronation. It was…a lot. And that is an understatement."

"It was." She let out a sigh. "No one believed me when I said I didn't know."

"Oh…" He'd not considered that. He should have. After all, everyone had known they were close. A few of his colleagues even assumed they were dating. He wasn't supposed to mention his title, hadn't figured anyone would ever say it in his presence again. But he still should have told her.

"What happened?" His chest was tight as he waited for her answer. He'd left her, focused on his family's wants. On their needs. Happy to be included, finally.

The reality that he wasn't really wanted had taken weeks to set in.

"Press. Questions I couldn't or wouldn't answer.

I even had a few agents reach out with suggestions for a tell-all book. One had already named it—*My Years with the Prince*."

Hazel laughed, the alto tones radiating through the night. "That was a tad much, as I told them."

"You could have made a lot of money on that story."

"Maybe." Hazel swung his hand and pulled him toward the festival, but she didn't let go. "But there wasn't a price I could put on our friendship. As far as blocking you, I had to get a new phone because someone gave my number to a tabloid. So… that's it."

"That's it." Syver pulled them to a stop again. He'd wasted so much time, and he wasn't wasting any more.

"At this rate, we'll miss the festival." Hazel smiled as she squeezed his hand. "Your favorite night only comes once a year."

"I don't care." And he meant it. Nothing mattered in this moment more than making sure she knew how deeply her words, her continued friendship, even when he hadn't known it, touched him. "Hazel…"

"Why did you come back?"

The question floored him. How could she not know? "Like I said, for you." He swallowed as the enormity of those words settled around them.

"For me?" Her face shifted in the late evening sun. This time of year, the sun didn't set until well after ten, and he was so glad he could see her features clearly.

She was stunned…shocked, and the revelation broke his heart. "Of course. I had this grand plan that you'd come to Fönn. That I'd convince you to leave London behind and join me at the pediatric hospital. We had a mass emigration issue under King Eirvin. Our medical professionals…well, we're still rebuilding."

It was his primary focus—but it wasn't the reason he'd come for her.

He shook his head. "No. That's not right?" He didn't want any misunderstanding.

"No, you didn't come for me to help Fönn?" He heard the tint of concern in her voice.

Syver would not let that stand. "I came because I wanted you with me." He'd thought he'd wanted his friend here. That was part of it, but he'd had other friends, other colleagues, who'd have helped Fönn. He'd not reached out to a single one.

It was Hazel he needed. And he was starting to suspect the feelings he'd associated with friendship were so much deeper even then.

"Oh." Her mouth formed a delicate O as she stared at him. "I'd have come."

The world disappeared as she held his gaze. For so long, he'd assumed she'd been angry. Rightfully so. Assumed she'd run and blocked him. And he'd lost years.

Years…

"Hazel." He lifted his free hand, let his thumb run along her chin. The cord he felt linking them clanged as her breath hitched. Whatever this was, was like nothing he'd felt before. "Hazel."

"You already said my name." She laughed and leaned her cheek against his hand.

"Prince Syver!" The call broke the spell between them.

She pulled back, but he squeezed the hand she still held. If she wanted him to let go, he would, but his heart soared when she squeezed back.

"Are you heading to the festival?" The young lad called as his mother tried to push him along, her eyes clearly understanding that he'd interrupted an important moment.

"Sorry!" She held up her hand, pushing her son, who couldn't be over seven.

"Why are you sorry, Mama?" He waved at Prince Syver. "We're going to the festival, but not for very long because I have to go to bed."

Hazel covered her mouth, but it didn't hide the sound of her giggle. "Yes, we are heading for the festival." Her words were bright, and she pulled at his hand, so they started walking toward the festival, too.

"We'll see you there," Syver called, grinning as the little boy skipped beside his mother.

The interaction was cute and would make anyone smile. But it was the woman still holding his hand that made his body sing.

CHAPTER FOUR

THE LAST LIGHTS of the festival dimmed, and night seemed to sigh in inky darkness. Meg had attended each night of the festival last year, and said she found something sad about the last night. The lights going out across the field, the closed shops. She'd lamented that there was nothing to signify the end besides the lights.

No closing ceremony. No celebration. Just darkness.

Hazel hadn't known what to expect. It wasn't a traditional festival environment. But she saw nothing sad about the dimming lights. It was an acknowledgment that this cycle of time was over and another was on the horizon.

Her eyes found the man beside her. Another shift. One she wanted.

He'd come for her five years ago. He'd wanted her here. With him.

The piece of her heart that had broken when she'd stood alone in their flat healed tonight.

She couldn't have stayed at the flat. People got past the doorman for three weeks straight. He'd always feign surprise or anger, but she knew the reporters were sliding him a few hundred dollars for access.

Hazel did not rate the same level of security as the wealthy residents and a prince. The once friendly looks of her neighbors had turned into nosey questions, followed by icy glares when they realized she wouldn't offer any gossip.

Leaving was the right answer, but she could have left a note. Something to let him know where she was. Maybe she would have, but she'd figured he'd ghosted her like so many others.

A miscommunication that they'd both been too hurt to reach out after. Humans really could make a muck of things.

Tonight, under the setting lights, the last of the heaviness between them lightened. Now there was no way to ignore the tension, the desire and the need left unbridled in its absence.

He'd nearly kissed her. That was where the moment was headed when the child interrupted them.

It would be easy to pretend she didn't know where this evening was heading. Once upon a time Hazel would have. But she wasn't conflicted. Hazel knew what she wanted.

His touch. The feel of his lips on hers. Syver. *Prince.*

The title hung in her mind. Hazel had accomplished much in her life. On her own. But there was no hidden aristocratic link in her bloodline. She'd be seen as lesser—always.

Yet, she didn't want to walk away. After five years without him, she couldn't do that.

"Do you ever tire of being a prince?" She hadn't meant to ask the question. She'd wanted to walk with him, spend the rest of the night with him. Kiss him.

But that title. The one that had hung over them since the day he disappeared. It raised questions. Ones that needed answering.

"Yes. It's something I had no control over, something that still creates." He paused, wrapping an arm around her waist.

"Creates?"

"Tension." His lips brushed the top of her head. But it was a passing caress, one that didn't quite feel like a kiss. "But tonight, I'm just Syver."

Just Syver.

That was nice. Even if she wasn't sure it was possible. However, it was nice to pretend that they'd stepped back in time. That here and now it was just Hazel and Syver.

"So, just Syver, what now?" It was an open-ended question. He could answer for tonight, could answer for the almost kiss they'd nearly shared, for the friction building between them.

Or in a flippant way, one they could laugh off tomorrow.

"Well, we have a few options." He leaned his head against hers and the feeling she'd had all those years ago of safety and security rammed back into place.

Were we just too busy to realize our bond was more? Or naive? Or scared of ruining the brilliant friendship?

Perhaps it was a combination of all three. And time and distance had stolen their ability to ignore it.

"We can stay here for a while. The park is open until one, and neither of us has work tomorrow. We can walk through the gardens. At night, the rich floral scents reach toward the stars."

That sounded lovely, but her soul craved more.

He moved his head against hers and for a moment she thought he'd kiss the top of it. When that didn't happen, she feared he meant to let her go. Instinctively, she tightened her grip on his waist, then relaxed. If he let her go, he let her go.

She could handle it. She'd put the need away, even if she didn't want to.

Lifting her hand from his waist, he spun her into his arms. Her eyes were adjusting to the darkness. The last bits of space between them closing as her body shifted against him.

Her heartbeat echoed in her ears as she lifted her chin.

Kiss me.

The words were on the tip of her tongue, but she couldn't quite force them out. Instead, she heard a single word slip out, "Or?"

"Or…" he bent his head, his breath warm against her ear as he whispered "…I kiss you."

"Kiss me." She wrapped her arms around his neck, pulling him to her. This might be a mistake, but she didn't care. She needed him.

Her lips met his in the darkness. The scent of

summer flowers wrapping around them. If Hazel thought this moment would dampen the desire she'd felt building since she'd first seen him, the reality was so much hotter.

She arched against him, oblivious to everything but her body's desperate urge. Her soul cried out, ages of longing seeming to rush forth.

His lips were soft, but his hands on her back were firm. Holding her in place, cradling her as he tasted her. A small slice of heaven she never wanted to leave.

"Hazel." Her name, whispered in Syver's deep tone, sent tingles floating from the tip of her head to the tips of her toes. If one could see happiness vibrate, she'd light up the entire festival site.

"Syver." She leaned her head against his shoulder. Everything shifted tonight. If she was honest, things had nearly shifted in their friendship before. A look here, a touch that lasted a hair too long. But they'd never crossed the invisible barrier. Never even acknowledged its presence.

Because there was no turning back now.

Once you kissed your best friend, the friendship you'd had, no matter how good, how strong, evaporated. In its place was something new.

Now they needed to figure out what that was. Or they could let it slide away into the night's oblivion.

She waited a minute, but when he said nothing, the nerves that lit when his lips met hers turned on her mind. Why wasn't he talking or kissing her… or something?

"We don't have to talk about it, if you don't want to." She hated those words. But if this was just a onetime thing, an impulsive action to break the fission between them…

"And if I want to talk about it?" Syver dropped a light kiss on her forehead, then another on her cheek. "If I want to talk about it very badly?"

She giggled, then felt ridiculous. She was not a teen or some girl lovesick for the first time. "Here or at your place—or mine?"

"Yours might be easier."

"Of course." She pursed her lips, hoping the darkness covered the wave of uncomfortableness beating against her mind. She wasn't exactly sure where Syver lived. That was something none of the blogs she'd followed ever mentioned—for good reasons.

Whether it was the palace grounds or someplace else, it certainly wasn't a one-bedroom furnished apartment. A place that would highlight how much social distance there was between them.

She'd made the place as homey as possible, but it still looked temporary. Certainly not like a place where'd you'd find royalty.

"What are you thinking? I can practically hear the mental jumps echoing in the night."

"How?" Issuing the challenge was easier than admitting she was worried her flat was lackluster. *Although I loved it when I got here.*

It was twice the size of her London rental, and didn't come with a grumpy old landlord who lived upstairs and monitored her comings and goings. Not that there'd been much to monitor.

Syver pulled her hand from around his neck and ran a finger gently over her thumb, just below where the nail bed met the nail. "You were rubbing this. I suspect you wanted to pick it."

It honestly hadn't crossed her mind, but the habit was so ingrained she often only noticed the issue after she started bleeding.

"Having lived with me for two years gives you an unfair advantage." Her bottom lip popped up, and she reeled it back in. She was *not* pouting in this moment.

"It does." Syver chuckled. "And I enjoy the advantage. Hazel, there is no pressure here."

"I know. But it's silly."

"All the more reason to tell me." His lips pressed against her neck. If he was trying to distract her, it was working.

"My flat isn't exactly a palace, and it's not exactly fit for royalty."

She pushed against his chest, enjoying the playful grunt that echoed before he wrapped his arm around her waist.

"Hazel…" He squeezed her side. "I'm just Syver. *Except you aren't.*

Rather than voice that truth, she laid her head against his. "Well, then let's head for my place, just Syver."

* * *

Rationally, he knew he wasn't just Syver. He was the heir to the throne of Fönn. The full son of King Eirvin, beloved son and brother...at least as far as the public was concerned.

Though if everything continued well with Queen Signe's pregnancy, he wouldn't be the heir for much longer. He didn't mind that loss. But when Erik had his heir, would Syver have any place in the family? When the illusion wasn't needed, would he become even more of an outsider?

Was that even possible?

The constant worries were easier to set aside with Hazel in his arms. With her he could almost forget the royal family's baggage. He was simply a man infatuated with the woman beside him. His best friend.

He'd spent five years missing a part of himself. Had he realized it was Hazel he needed?

No.

Maybe he should have. Those two years with her were the best of his life. At least until they'd kissed tonight.

Even if he had realized it, he wouldn't have searched her out. That knowledge sucked. He'd thought she was gone when he found their flat empty.

Their flat.

That was how he'd always thought of it. The

week after Hazel moved in, it was theirs. And he'd left with a brief note. Left her unprotected.

And rather than monetize her fifteen minutes of fame, she'd changed her number and moved out of their flat. To protect him.

He wasn't sure what would happen next now that they'd kissed, but no matter what it was, he was protecting Hazel.

Always.

"Home sweet home," Hazel sighed as she pulled her keys from the small bag she'd carried tonight.

He could hear the tension in her tone, and her shoulders were tight. Over a flat?

Maybe he should have taken her back to the palace. But the head of security was a terror. Now that the Queen was almost through her second trimester, he'd tightened policies further.

Erik and Signe have suffered three miscarriages. Few knew of their upcoming bundle of joy. And the country wouldn't know until she was past twenty-four weeks.

That meant Arne, the head of security, wasn't letting anyone pass, even Syver's guests, without at least a minimal check.

Arne was dismissive of Syver, like most of the staff. Everyone knew Erik didn't give Syver much responsibility, so he was overlooked. The man wouldn't go out of his way for Syver.

It was selfish, but he didn't want any delay. He

wanted to talk to Hazel. Wanted to kiss her again. Spend time with her.

"Darling," he kissed the back of her neck, "if you want to go to the palace…"

"No." She opened the door and pulled him into her home.

He was not prepared for the rush of emotions as he stepped into Hazel's flat. There were house plants tucked into the small bookcase. And a vining plant hanging over a shelf on the opposite wall, a soft-looking blue blanket on the back of the couch and a romance novel on the small table by it.

It was like stepping back in time. Coming home.

"I see you found the garden center." He'd joked that their flat in London was half greenhouse. And he'd loved watching her care for plants. He'd even gotten her one of the vine-type ones…though he couldn't remember the type now.

She looked at the plants, then shook her head. "No. You'll have to show me where it is!"

The squeal was music to his heart. The woman loved plants, and he'd enjoyed seeing her baby them.

"These are the ones that were hardy enough to make the journey and fine with customs. I packed their box carefully, then told them what to expect. I've babied them this week. They are bouncing back from the stress." She was smiling, but her face was quite serious.

Her plants were her babies. She could chat about any green thing. Plant talk with Hazel, he'd called it.

Another thing I missed without knowing it.

"You brought the plants?"

"Only a few. I gave the rest to the staff I knew liked plants. But berry arrowheads and pothos are hardy. Remember, the employee told you there was nothing you could do to kill this one?" She moved toward the trailing vine plant on the wall as his heart exploded.

"You kept the plant I got you?" Kept it, nurtured it and brought it to Fönn. There wasn't a good definition for the emotions seeing the plant sent through his chest. A plant…his gift to her.

"It lost a few vines on the way, but a little trim and he was good as new." Hazel shrugged. "I'd never be able to part with it."

"Hazel…" There were so many things to say. But the emotions tumbling through him caught all the words. He'd gotten the plant as a baby green. The garden center employee had sworn that if she didn't like it, it was easy to care for. That if she went on holiday, he'd be able to manage it.

And now it was here. In Fönn. A piece of their past to start their future.

"I couldn't leave it, Syver." She swallowed and shrugged. "I know it's only a plant, but you got it for me."

"I missed you, Hazel. Every single day." There

were many things to say, but he needed her to know this most.

Her lips brushed his, the touch brief, but it ignited a flame in his body.

"Do you think we missed signs of..." Hazel pursed her lips, then leaned her head against his shoulder.

"Of this?" He kissed the top of her head, loving the feel of her in his arms again. They'd sworn they were just friends to everyone. Sworn they were roommates, nothing more.

Maybe they'd even believed it.

But he had dated no one while they lived together...and neither had she. They had reserved their free time for movies, garden center dates, walks in the park and her helping him study for exams.

"Yes." They weren't looking for it, and maybe it wasn't the right time then. But they'd certainly missed the signals.

Or willfully ignored them.

She looked up, and he kissed her cheek, then moved his lips to her jaw until he caught her lips.

Hazel. His world had been busy, but it wasn't until she'd walked back into his life last week that he'd realized how empty it was.

She tasted of honey cakes, pleasure and home. His fingers cradled her neck as he explored her mouth. If there was a more perfect moment, he didn't want to find it.

Pulling back, Hazel looked over her shoulder. "It's nearly one."

They'd said they were going back to her place, but he wasn't sure either of them had realized just how late it was. Wrapped up in each other it was easy to miss.

"Should I go?" There were things to say, conversations to have, but it was late. And he wanted time with her.

"You could stay. We can watch a movie, just be together. I've missed just being together." She bit her lip, "I'm not ready for…for…"

Her cheeks blazed and then she nodded, seemingly to herself. "I'm not ready to go to bed with you, but I also am not ready to end tonight. But if you want to leave—"

"A movie sounds perfect." Syver sighed as the rightness of this moment settled with him. A movie with Hazel. "Where's the television?"

"Oh." She looked around and then ran a hand over her thumb before pointing to the door that had to be her bedroom. "Is that a problem?"

"Nope." Did he want her? *Yes.* Crave her touch? *Absolutely.* But she'd left her home a week ago, gone through so many changes all at once. He'd wait however long it took for her to be ready.

CHAPTER FIVE

HAZEL STIRRED THE cinnamon batter and made sure the griddle was warming. Crepes on her day off was a tradition she'd started when she'd lived with Charlotte. Her roommate, who'd met the love of her life on holiday and married on a whim, then needed Hazel to find new lodgings.

Their love story, which now included the cutest set of twins, was the reason she was fixing cinnamon crepes with an apple butter filling for Syver this morning.

Hazel ran her fingers over her lips. Part of her couldn't believe she'd kissed him last night, and woken fully clothed in his arms this morning.

How had they waited so long to kiss?

She'd fallen asleep before the movie they'd selected finished. Then woken to Syver holding her. He'd taken his jumper off, but stayed by her side all night.

That was not something Alec would have done. Particularly after she'd indicated she had no plans to sleep with him.

She wanted to. Wanted to kiss her way down Syver's body. Wanted to hold him tight and do things her mind had conjured quite freely in her dreams.

But for all the friendship and heat between them, they were still strangers in some ways. There were things to say. Things she hadn't wanted to broach so late and when they were both drunk on the emotional high of first kisses.

This morning, with crepes and coffee, it was time.

"That smells delicious. Cinnamon crepes. I haven't had those since I left London."

"Syver!" He'd been sleeping so soundly, she thought she had a few more minutes to get her thoughts together. She turned and some of the batter dropped off the spoon. "Shoot!" Setting the bowl aside, she reached for a towel, but Syver's hand caught hers.

"Hazel." His hand was warm in hers, but the batter was spreading and her cheeks were hot. Nothing like not getting all your mental insecurities set aside before coffee.

He ignored the batter.

"The floor will be sticky."

"I'll clean it." He slipped a hand under her chin, his blue eyes holding hers. "But are you all right? It's not like you to be so jumpy."

"Nervous. There are," she gestured between them, "things to say."

"There are. But I'm so glad I'm here." He grinned then dropped his mouth to hers. Her heartbeat echoed in her ears as her body flushed with need and excitement. This was what her soul craved.

She pulled back, mostly because the smell of the first burned crepe circled them. "Always burn the first one, right?" She moved to grab the pastry off the griddle and turned to find Syver scooping up the dropped batter in the towel.

He stepped to the sink, dropped the towel in, then wet another and cleaned the mess.

Mist covered her eyes. It was such a simple task. It shouldn't make her heart race or her eyes water. But Alec never did anything for her.

And her mother...

Hazel got things done. Because no one was coming to her rescue.

And now there was a literal prince cleaning up the floor in her rented flat.

"Hey," Syver slid his arm around her waist. His fingers brushed across her back as he laid his head against hers. "What's wrong?"

"Nothing." She felt the uncomfortable laugh before she heard it. Nothing was wrong. "I just can't believe a prince cleaned my floor."

"Just Syver here."

This was the other thing they needed to discuss. Because whether he wanted to admit it made him different or not, Syver was the heir to the throne. Her throat tightened, but she needed to make sure she understood the requirements, the expectations, the rules that came with dating him.

Because Hazel didn't want to mess this up.

"I promise that when you are here or we're alone, you will be just Syver. But you are the heir to the throne. You are Prince Syver and I'm just Hazel."

"There's nothing *just* about you, Hazel." She saw an emotion dance across his eyes that she worried for a moment was anger. It was fleeting, and she didn't think it was directed at her, but she leaned back.

A force of habit from watching Alec and adjusting to his moods for so long.

"What was that?" Syver tilted his head.

"What?"

"You moved away from me. I was frustrated because..." He threw his hands up, took a breath then nodded, like he was mentally arguing with himself. "I came home because my family wanted me to. But my relationship with them...is still strained."

"I'm sorry." She hated that for him. Family was supposed to be your safe place, but for so many it wasn't.

"Family is a frustration point for me, but that has nothing to do with you. So again...why did you lean back?"

She could see the questions in his eyes. Hazel turned, focusing on the crepe, trying to ignore the mist coating her eyes.

"Why did you come to Fönn?"

"Honestly?"

He slipped beside her and leaned against the counter. "I think honesty is best."

"Fönn was the first offer I got. And I needed to leave. I was in a relationship...it wasn't good." That was such an understatement. "He wasn't physically abusive, but I got good at reading the signs that would set him off. And I can read you so well because we lived together." She chuckled, trying to lighten the mood. Alec was her past. But the hints of it were still with her, whether she wanted them to be or not.

"Hazel." He closed his eyes then put his arm around her waist. When he opened his eyes, he sighed, "I hate that you went through that."

"Me, too." She wouldn't offer the statement that it had made her stronger. In some ways maybe it had. But the truth was that it was a period of her life she didn't like looking at. If she could undo it, she would.

She dropped the crepes onto plates. "How about we move to the table? So coming home wasn't what you expected?"

"No." Syver cut into the crepe. "I love my family. I work hard for the royal family, but it never feels like enough. Which is why I like being just Syver." He winked.

Hazel wanted him to be just Syver, but that wasn't the life he'd been born into. And they couldn't simply ignore it.

"We can be just Syver and Hazel here, or even at work, but you are a prince…and with us…" She picked up the mug of coffee she'd poured early wishing there was more heat coming through ceramic. A way to push away the fear. "I'm about as far from aristocratic as possible. *When* we tell people, they will have opinions." She'd experienced that, seen the looks, heard the questions. The media this time would be more direct.

It changed things.

"When? You want to hide me?" Syver pushed his chair back. His tone was light, like he was trying to make a joke, but it felt flat.

That tore through her. She wanted to scream from the top of Fönn's mountains that she was dating Syver. But what if this was a temporary thing? A fling that burned out.

It didn't feel like that...but she'd misread signs before. If this burned brightly only for days...well, it would break her heart and she didn't want others to see that.

Not again.

"What if this is just a fling?" That had come out wrong. Her brain refused to behave this morning. The last thing she wanted was to cheapen what she suspected was between them.

"It's not." Syver's tone was soft, but authoritative.

There's the Prince.

The person so certain of their position in life that they could make declarations.

A foreign idea to Hazel. Her position had never been certain, even when she thought it was. Dating a prince, falling for one. It changed everything.

"What is your worry, sweetheart? Tell me. I can handle it."

The urge to rub her thumb pulled at her. She

didn't want to hurt him, but she'd lost so much before. She took a deep breath and leaped. "There were so many questions when you left. They'll be questions again."

"Ones we get to answer together."

Together.

She wouldn't stand alone this time. He'd be by her side.

That didn't mean the questions wouldn't be direct or things they didn't want to answer. "Is it too much to ask for a few weeks of quiet before the show gets underway?"

"No, it isn't. We can wait until you're ready for anything." Syver made sure she was looking at him. "Provided you understand, I'm not hiding you. The second you want the King to know or Meg, or the universe, you tell me. And I will shout it to the heavens."

She opened her mouth, but no words came out. How did you respond to that? No one had ever wanted to shout to the next block, let alone to the universe, that they were with her. Syver's certainty, his unwavering tone, shot electricity through her.

"I missed having breakfast with you." She reached for his hand across the table.

"I missed everything about you."

"Your clothes are here." Hazel smiled as she held up the bag the palace aid had dropped off.

"Thanks," he kissed her cheek, "I'm going to

hop in the shower. Pop some popcorn for the next movie. Your choice."

She smiled as he headed down the hallway. They'd spent the day laughing, catching up, talking and bingeing the movies they'd missed together. It was silly and the perfect way to spend a day.

She hummed as she started the popcorn maker.

"Is there anything that smells as good as popcorn?" Syver asked.

Hazel turned, "That was a fast shower." The words were barely out of her mouth before it started watering as she stared at the gorgeous man at the entrance to her kitchen.

After his shower, a little water dripped from his head and the tight white undershirt he wore hugged all the right places. He stepped to her, dropped a kiss on her cheek, but it wasn't enough. Popcorn and movies were distant memories as Hazel wrapped her arms around him and claimed his mouth. Syver's tongue met hers and the electricity his body ignited exploded. Her hips rubbed against his as she molded to him.

"Syver?"

His lips trailed along her chin as his fingers rubbed her lower back. "Yes?"

"You want to watch another movie?" She looked at the popcorn. If he wanted more time, that was fine, but she wanted him. All of him, now.

"I want what you want." His mouth met hers and

their tongues danced, meeting each other's rhythms as though they'd done this thousands of times. "If that's a movie, fine…if not."

His fingers slipped under her shirt and ran along her belly.

"You have a way with words, Syver."

"Wait until you see what else I can do with my mouth."

Syver picked her up, and Hazel let out a small gasp. This felt a little fairytale-ish. And she loved it!

Hazel felt perfect in his arms as Syver headed back toward her bed. He wanted to shout to the world that this woman was his.

Syver wasn't sure how his mother and brother would take it. But that was a problem for another day.

"Syver," Hazel breathed his name, and his heart nearly melted.

"You are so beautiful." He nipped her ear before laying her on the bed. "So incredibly beautiful."

Her cheeks darkened, and he ached to know if the rest of her body turned to rose when she received a compliment.

After lifting her shirt to just below her breasts, he pressed his lips to her belly, loving the small hitch she gave when he lowered his attention to just below her waist. The urge to strip her quickly warred deep inside.

But Syver refused to rush this moment with

Hazel. He planned to worship her body with his mouth, with his tongue, with his hands. With his whole being.

Her hands skimmed across his head, catching bits of his hair as she moaned his name. His manhood was already aching for release. "Hazel," he sighed her name as he finished lifting her shirt over her head, then watched, mesmerized as she unhooked her bra. "You're so beautiful."

"You already said that." She bit her lip, and he watched the skin on her chest shift to a rose hue as she reached for him.

"It bears repeating." He raised his hand, running a finger along her breasts, circling one nipple, watching it tighten on his touch.

After dipping his head, he let his mouth follow the same path. Suckling her, enjoying the feel of her in his mouth as his fingers slipped her comfy pants down.

She wore no undergarments beneath them.

Dear God, his body was quaking with a yearning he'd never felt so acutely.

His hand ran over her bare bottom and even if he'd wanted to, he couldn't stop his exhale. "I imagined stripping your knickers down all day, but this. This is so much better, Hazel."

"I never wear them with my cotton pants." She let out a small giggle as her hand reached under his shirt. Each touch lighting a flame on his skin.

"That is information I will file away for future

reference." He lifted his arms, letting Hazel remove his shirt.

Before her, he'd have never said that stripping clothing off piece by piece was foreplay. Sure, it was exciting, but the ache he got watching a naked Hazel lift his shirt, unbutton his pants and slip them over his hips was something he'd never experienced.

Her soft hands ran along his length and his groan echoed in the room. His body shuddered; he wanted to bury himself in her, hold her as he drove into her. But he was determined she'd remember their first time as more than his frantic need for her.

Lifting her hand, he then kissed the fingers that had stroked him. "I want you, Hazel, desperately."

"The feeling is very mutual, Syver."

She was a siren, with curly hair, hazel eyes and a voice that drove him to the edge. But he was not too far gone yet. "Lay back."

Hazel raised an eyebrow, and for a moment he thought she'd balk at the request. Instead, she leaned herself against her pillows.

He followed her, captured her mouth, enjoying the taste of her against his tongue before he slid his way down her body.

Arousal chased him as he drank her in. After lowering his mouth to her mound, he flicked his tongue against her pleasure bud, loving the sound of his name floating in the room. Her hips arched, offering herself fully to him.

Yes.

Syver gripped her backside, keeping her in the perfect place for his mouth to worship her. Her hands wrapped through his hair, and he heard her breath accelerate.

He wanted, needed, to push her over oblivion's edge. Hazel, his Hazel.

"Syver!" Her pant was music to his ears as her body softened following her orgasm.

He kissed the inside of each of her thighs as he kissed his way back up her body.

She shifted and pulled open the top drawer of her bedside table. He followed her hand, before grabbing the condom and then ripping it open as quickly as possible. Syver needed her now.

He sheathed himself, then joined their bodies.

"Syver!" Hazel wrapped her legs around him. Her body matching each of his strokes.

Time slowed, then stopped, as they gave in to their desires. He dropped kisses on her cheek, then her jaw before joining their lips.

Her fingers traced down his back as she met each of his thrusts. They claimed each other. It was magical and so normal. Her body tightened again, and he kissed her as he finally gave in to his own climax.

He was right where he was supposed to be. It was a feeling he only truly got with Hazel.

CHAPTER SIX

HAZEL LOOKED AT SYVER, then forced her gaze back to the tablet chart in front of her. It was a slow day. Which normally she'd be grateful for. After all, one didn't really want the children's emergency department overrun with chaos.

But with a little activity, she might be able to keep her eyes from wandering to him. They'd spent the last few days cocooned in her apartment. Reminiscing, exploring each other's body and relaxing.

He'd even had groceries delivered so they didn't have to leave. There were more than a few perks to wearing the crown.

She wasn't prepared to tell anyone that she was dating the Prince just yet. Wasn't ready to explain or face the questions she knew were coming. The pictures, the looks.

She'd had most of them thrown at her when he'd left. She could answer them this time. Say aloud that she was dating Syver. That the man she was with made song lyrics make sense. He made her chest heavy with joy instead of worry, made her feel like herself. All better than great things!

Maybe it was selfish, but she wanted some time to revel in those feelings without the world dissecting it.

And she wanted to be sure. Maybe that wasn't

fair, but after Alec…she just needed more than one blissful weekend.

"So did you have a good weekend?" Meg stepped beside Hazel, her eyes looking toward the office doctors used during slow moments. The door where Syver had disappeared only a few minutes before.

There was a hint of curiosity in her tone. The American nurse was friendly, bubbly…heck, she could step onto a set and play the role of friendly nurse without having to try at all. She was also incredibly observant.

Luckily, it was also easy to distract her.

"Tell me about your engagement party." The event wasn't for another few months, but Meg was already planning…with folders and binders outlining everything.

Hazel wanted a wedding, one day. But Meg's level of planning was epic. If this was the organization for the engagement party, Hazel wasn't sure what it'd look like when it was time to plan the actual nuptials.

"Oh! I found the perfect bakery to make the cupcakes. They can do the design Lev wants. A historical re-creation of Fönn's pastries. Historians."

Hazel laughed. Lev was a university historian specializing in Fönn's history. Meg said she'd learned a lot from him, but it wasn't the cake's decor that mattered, not really.

"I'm sure they'll be beautiful. But what will they taste like?"

Meg clapped and closed her eyes like she was remembering the flavors. "Lemon raspberry cake with the lightest frosting. I ate three of them, and my fiancé, I love saying that…" She practically swooned as she repeated the word. "My *fiancé*!"

"It is a fun word." Her mother had gotten engaged three times. It had never worked out.

That hadn't stopped Hazel from dreaming of her own. Imagining the man who'd stand by the altar and choose her.

"Anyway, my fiancé ate four. Luckily, they were tiny tasting ones, but there was no doubt which we'd choose." She grinned and launched into a list of items she'd checked off her ever-growing to-do list over the last few days.

Hazel smiled and nodded at the right times, keeping her eyes focused away from the door where Syver was working.

"So, now that I have explained everything about my party," Meg hit Hazel's hip with hers, "you can tell me all about your days off." She winked and laughed. "Why won't you talk about your weekend? I can keep a secret."

"I spent the weekend cocooned in my apartment. It was lovely, but not nearly as exciting as engagement planning." They'd never left, though lying in Syver's arms was more exciting than party planning in Hazel's opinion.

Syver stepped out of the office, and Hazel's eyes lifted automatically before dropping back to Meg.

Meg sighed and looked at the patient area where Syver had disappeared. She met Hazel's gaze, took a breath, then looked over her shoulder again and sighed.

"Something to say?" Hazel probably shouldn't issue the challenge, but it was clear Meg wanted to say something.

"He's different since you arrived." She smiled. "Well, honestly, he's been different since your résumé landed."

Hazel was proud that she didn't make a face. She'd proven herself over the last week. Even if Syver hadn't put in a good word for her, she was the best choice for this position.

But it was the first part of the statement that perked her curiosity. "How is Dr. Bernhardt different?"

Maybe she shouldn't ask, but…well, curiosity was a natural human trait.

"He's happy."

Hazel couldn't stop the spread of her smile. Happy. Five little letters in one word that made her heart sing.

"He wasn't unhappy before, but he was apart. Almost going through the motions. Like he was missing something. And I think he was missing…you."

Hazel's mouth opened, but she couldn't force any words out.

"What are you two discussing?" Syver's words broke the spell holding Hazel.

She'd spent all morning tracking his movements, but Meg's words had transfixed her.

"Engagement planning!" Meg offered. "I found the perfect cake. Now I need to find the best flowers."

"Good luck." Syver smiled, but a bit of the light dimmed behind his eyes.

"What do you think?" Meg leaned on the desk, her face bright. "After all, you're from Fönn. The party is in autumn, any recommendations?"

Syver looked at the chart he was carrying, "I've no idea what might be right for an engagement party or wedding, Meg. Even if I planned to wed, the palace would make all the choices."

Her breath caught, and she saw Meg's head swivel to her. Syver didn't look up, though.

Even if I planned to wed.

Those words shocked her, but it was the other part that hammered home who she was dating. No choices? A royal wedding was a big deal, but it was still the bride and groom's day.

"You aren't ever planning on marrying?" Meg looked at her again, but Hazel didn't react.

Family doesn't have to mean marriage and a baby carriage. She knew that. Believed it. But marriage was a union between two people. Two, not a royal court. If he wasn't free to make choices on his wedding day, what else was he not free to do?

This was not the place for that discussion. But

the lines etched into the corners of his eyes worried her.

"Astrid, in Room Three, needs transferred to a room upstairs. The virus has dehydrated her and exhausted her system. A bag of fluids and observation for at least twenty-four hours are necessary. Her parents have done a great job monitoring her fluid intake, but she can't keep anything down. In a few days, the toddler will keep them on their toes again, but for now she needs admitted."

"I'll start the transfer." Meg pushed a button on her tablet and the orders started printing on the desk. She grabbed them and wandered off.

"So, what kind of cake is she getting?" Syver leaned forward, coffee, cinnamon and mint mixing in her nose as he grinned. Many people found it weird that medical professionals could shift so fast, but one had to learn to compartmentalize in this line of work, or you went mad.

"Lemon raspberry." She wanted to know about his previous statement. About his lack of control in his own life. And why he'd said it so confidently... in her presence.

That hurt more than she wanted to admit. What if the palace didn't approve of her? Would the King and Queen step in? And if they did, would Syver listen?

What were the signs she needed to watch for? Would she recognize them?

"Hazel—" His eyes softened, and he leaned as close as was professionally acceptable.

Before he could say anything else, a shout echoed in the bay. Hazel hated the sweep of relief passing through her. They'd spent a weekend together, agreed they weren't seeing anyone else, but that was a far cry from wanting to discuss wedding bells.

The finality of his tone unnerved her, but she'd focus on that later.

"Prince Syver, my daughter needs aid." A blonde beauty was helping her daughter walk in. The teen girl was holding up her foot, tears streaking down her face.

"Mia—" Syver answered.

"Dr. Bernhardt, Astrid is seizing," Meg called and Syver turned, racing toward the room.

She shouldn't have wished for more to do. Hazel met the mother's gaze. At least this emergency wasn't life-threatening. "Are you Mia?"

"No, I mean I am, but you can call me Lady Penve."

If this was a movie, Hazel was sure she'd be able to see Lady Penve's breath as her icy tone lashed out. "My daughter needs help. Why is Prince Syver rushing off?"

Hazel blinked. Meg's call had been distinct. Astrid was seizing. A rare complication for a virus, but one that needed to be taken seriously. Lady Penve's daughter had injured her foot.

Hazel wasn't sure how the injury occurred, but her foot wasn't bleeding profusely. She was in pain, but walking into the emergency room under her own powers. Therefore, she was a lower priority than a seizure.

A much lower priority. Something that shouldn't be hard to understand.

"Another patient has a medical situation." Hazel kept her tone even. Maybe Lady Penve didn't understand the implications of Meg's call. Even though Hazel wasn't sure how she could miss it.

"I heard. However, Hilda needs him." She crossed her arms and tapped her toe on the ground, a motion that was far too close to a cartoon villain.

Hazel had become a nurse at twenty-two and completed her ANP at twenty-eight. At thirty-two, she'd seen all sorts of patients and parents. Worry brought out the best in some, and the worst in many others.

"I'm here to help. So, Hilda, what happened?"

"I slipped outside—"

"She was climbing a tree when she's been told not to. And at your age. You should be past this!"

Hazel pursed her lips, biting back the urge to tell Lady Penve that Hilda was old enough to tell her the issue. The girl was a teenager, at least fifteen, maybe older. "Did you fall out of the tree and hurt your ankle?"

"No." Hilda's voice shook as she looked at her mother, then lifted her foot. A large stick was stuck in the center of her foot. "I landed wrong when I jumped down."

"And she was not wearing shoes."

"I see that." Hazel kept her tone light as she moved to grab a wheelchair. She hated to agree with Lady Penve when she was being so disrespectful, but if Hilda had worn shoes, this injury wouldn't have occurred.

Of course, as a child who'd loved to roam barefoot, Hazel also understood the desire to climb trees shoeless. It was a rite of passage. And teens were still children. In fact, in her experience, they were prone to rash decisions almost as often as toddlers.

"Let's get you into a room." Their triage nurse usually saw patients first, but Hazel could handle the stick removal. And she was loath to subject another staff member to the vitriol Lady Penve seemed intent on dispensing.

"When will Prince Syver be available?"

"Not sure." Hazel kept her words even. "The good news is, this is something I can treat."

"No. We'll wait for Prince Syver." Lady Penve crossed her arms.

"Mama…"

"We will wait." She gave her daughter a look Hazel knew Hilda had seen many times before.

It broke her heart and was a reminder that emotional trauma was not relegated to any class. Children learned parental behaviors…and how to survive them.

"I assure you, Lady Penve, that I am a qualified advanced nurse-practitioner. I am fully capable of numbing your daughter, pulling the stick out and assessing further needs."

Puncture wounds were delicate treatments. Depending how far the stick went into Hilda's foot, she might need the wound packed. And she needed antibiotics. The stick had a plethora of germs.

"The longer the stick is there, the greater the risk of infection."

"Something she should have considered before climbing the tree. You made the mistake and now you'll wait for Prince Syver."

Red danced across Hazel's vision. Being careful was a good reminder, but accidents happened. And delayed treatment was *not* an acceptable punishment. "How old are you?"

"Excuse me?" Lady Penve raised an eyebrow.

Hazel didn't acknowledge the interruption. In Fönn, children sixteen and older had rights in determining their medical care. Hilda was climbing trees, but she was clearly a teen.

"I turned sixteen last week."

"Sixteen and climbing trees."

The cutting remark didn't bother Hazel. It was the age she needed. "Hilda, I do not know when Dr. Bernhardt will be available. He is caring for a two-year-old with a virus who had a seizure after he asked for her to be admitted to the hospital. Your foot is not a priority for him. Do you understand?"

"I do." Her eyes slid to her mother, then back to Hazel. "Can you remove it?"

"I can."

"I said…" Lady Penve put both hands on her hips, straightening her shoulders. If she was hoping to intimidate Hazel, it wouldn't work. "*We* are waiting for Dr. Bernhardt."

"Your daughter has requested I remove the stick. As an ANP, I am more than qualified. At sixteen, she can choose her medical decisions. You can stay and remain quiet. Or you can leave."

"I will do neither!"

"There is a third option, and that is Security forcefully taking you from the room. Your choice." Hazel walked to the sink and washed her hands before donning gloves.

Lady Penve stormed from the room, and Hilda let out an audible breath. "She's probably going to talk to management." *And this isn't the first time.*

She didn't need to say the last words for Hazel to hear them. That wasn't her concern, though.

Directing her attention to Hilda, Hazel looked at the injury. The stick looked to have gone straight into her foot. The surrounding area was red, but the puncture wound was contained. The stick in her foot hurt, but the sixteen-year-old now had another big choice to make. "Let's worry about the problem sticking out of your foot right now."

Hilda looked down at her foot, glared at the stick, then looked to Hazel. "How?"

"I can numb your foot with lidocaine."

"That is going to burn." Hilda pursed her lips and wiped a tear from her cheek as she interrupted. "My friend had an accident on his yacht last summer. He needed over thirty stitches and swore the lidocaine hurt worse than anything."

"Some people describe it as a powerful bee sting, others like lightning. I don't know what your sensation will be. The other option is I can take the stick out quickly without numbing it. I've done a similar procedure before. Once it's out, I will pack the wound and put a local numbing cream on it."

"Both are going to hurt." Hilda's voice trembled, but she didn't look away from Hazel.

"Yes." This situation would require a large dose to make sure she was numb. The odds of a negative reaction went up exponentially with the amount needed for the procedure.

It was Hilda's choice. Hazel would do whatever her patient wished.

Gripping the table, Hilda nodded. "Pull it out."

Hazel didn't wait.

"Prince Syver!"

Syver wiped his face clear of emotion as he turned to greet Mia, Lady Penve. Astrid was stable, but whenever a patient was struggling, it was difficult for Syver. The plan to transfer her to a regular room had shifted to transfer to the intensive care unit. Three words he hated telling parents.

It was best, and temporary. That didn't change the emotions the unit shift brought.

He needed a few minutes to decompress, but that was apparently not happening. "Mia—"

She didn't wait for his greeting. "I need you to do something about your nurse."

Of course, she had a complaint. Mia was difficult, and that was the nicest descriptor he could give. The woman exuded the attitude King Eirvin's focus on the aristocracy had fostered. She and a group of her friends had floated the idea of a private hospital so their children didn't have to wait.

It was technically part of Erik's Health Initiative. An initiative Syver had offered to aid multiple times. One his mother had lobbied for his participation in. Only for them to be turned down repeatedly. At least his brother hadn't followed through with the private hospital expenditure.

It was bad enough when the aristocracy felt the country owed them special treatment. But wanting a hospital staffed with the best doctors when the rest of the country needed quality medical care—was horrid.

Syver had urged Erik to kill the idea as soon as he ascended the throne. He'd delayed the request rather than remove it. And Erik made sure the aristocracy knew the delay was Syver's recommendation.

If there was bad press to take, or a policy Erik didn't think his sycophants would like, it fell on the imposter heir. That recommendation had earned him a few enemies, but Syver didn't care.

"*I* don't have any nurses, Mia." He pinched the bridge of his nose, knowing the stress indicator would have no impact on Mia's tirade.

Ensuring his voice was level, Syver started an explanation he only planned to deliver once. "Our human resources department hires the finest staff—I have no control over it."

That was mostly true, but he knew people listened when he talked. Because his voice held more weight than it should, he was cautious about how he used it.

"I want Nurse Hazel Simpson fired."

"Not happening." He folded his arms as he leaned against the counter. He didn't know what had occurred with Mia and her daughter, but he knew Hazel would never do something not in the best interest of her patient.

Mia opened her mouth, and Syver held up his hand. "What happened to Hilda?"

"She had a stick in her foot, climbing a tree. I swear she's intent on making a spectacle of herself." Mia crossed her arms and took a deep breath. She'd been trained from an early age that one did not lose their cool in public.

She was failing now, which was only making her angrier. He knew she was trying to rein the emotions in, trying to gain control so she could exude the cool calmness expected of her.

It was unfair that Mia had internalized that toxic belief and unfair that her daughter was growing up in the same environment. But life at its core was unfair and the thing one controlled least was the status of their birth.

"Hazel didn't remove the stick?" Syver felt the yawn at the back of his throat and looked down, trying to catch it.

"I did." Hazel was smiling as she joined their little band, but it didn't reach her eyes. It was the "customer service" grin medical professionals learned to wear with difficult patients or family members. "Your daughter is asking after you."

Mia looked at Hazel, judgement radiating from her upturned nose. "I wanted Prince Syver to remove the stick."

"And your daughter requested I not wait for Dr. Bernhardt as he treated a higher priority case."

"Higher priority." Mia's left eye twitched. "My daughter is a member of the aristocracy."

"Yes, you indicated that, Lady Penve, but once you cross the emergency department threshold, patient priority becomes who needs care the most, not a class distinction." Hazel's eyes held unsaid words.

"I packed Hilda's foot. The puncture wound is just under half an inch. I prescribed antibiotics and showed her how to clean it. Do you want to see the wound before I start the discharge papers?"

"No." Syver shook his head and saw Mia's hands vibrate before she stepped between them.

"You will look at my daughter before this nurse discharges her. I do not trust her. Besides, Hilda deserves to have someone like you look at her."

Hazel blinked but didn't respond. All medical professionals had patients or parents of patients challenge them. Sometimes it was the right move. But this was pure classism.

"I can contact your brother if needed."

That was an argument she could have used with the former King—successfully. King Erik didn't deal with medical issues; that didn't mean he wouldn't hear the complaint. Didn't mean he wouldn't use it against Syver.

The reason he'd called Syver home was to have an adviser on this issue. Syver understood the problem. Erik rarely listened. But when he did, when Syver could make a real difference, it made his return to Fönn worth it.

And eventually he'd earn a full place. He believed that, somehow, Erik would see the wisdom in hearing his counsel. In treating him like a brother. A real brother.

"I want it known that I trust Hazel, and all the nursing and medical staff employed here, Mia. Go ahead with the discharge papers, Hazel."

Hazel started toward the nurses' station, returning a few minutes later with the discharge papers. "I'll take a quick look at Hilda, then should you have questions…"

"My sister has your number. She still talks about you."

Syver caught Hazel's shoulders shift, but he didn't look her way. He'd dated Mia's youngest sister months ago. And *dated* was a very loose term for the two dates they'd gone on before he'd told her he didn't see a relationship developing.

"You need to call the hospital or Hilda's pediatrician, if you have questions."

Mia released a sound that was not an agreement as she followed him to see Hilda. The woman was demanding, but she wasn't the first demanding countess he'd dealt with.

And she won't be the last...

Syver had never monitored the clock on a shift. The hospital and his patients were always his primary focus. In fact, his mentor had instructed him to remember that burnout was possible for anyone, and time away from the hospital was a good thing.

Today, though...today he watched the hands tick toward six.

"If you glare at that clock any harder, it might slow just to spite you." Hazel moved beside him, her presence bringing a wave of calm.

He let out the breath he knew he'd been holding. His shoulders loosened and a bit of the day's drama drifted away.

"Ride home with me?" The words escaped, and he wouldn't recall them even if he could.

He wanted to spend time with Hazel, wanted her beside him.

"Syver…" She'd taken public transportation this morning, not wanting to add to gossip if anyone saw them arriving together.

He had a change of clothes at her house and was planning to head directly there, but he didn't want to spend the extra few minutes away from her.

"I know what you are going to say. Know the thought process behind it, I even understand. But we've both had a rough day. Let me drive you home." He kept the words even so that if someone heard, she could claim he was just being a good friend.

Friend.

He'd associated that word with Hazel from the first day they'd met. Now though…after spending the weekend in her arms. After waking beside her, holding her…it was such a small part of what he wanted to call her.

What he wanted was to shout to the world about her. Let them know about the woman who'd chosen him.

"Let Prince Syver take you home. The bus will add at least another thirty minutes to your commute. And after Lady Penve…" Meg's voice rose an octave as she crossed her arms and pressed her lips closed.

The woman had railed, even as Hilda had walked out of the hospital. Meg had spent most of the day with Astrid and her parents—ensuring the toddler was stable before the transfer.

Meg had had a few choice words for Mia…all muttered under her breath but loud enough for Syver and Hazel to hear.

"If you're sure you don't mind?"

"Oh, he doesn't mind." Meg waved goodbye and started out the door.

"I think she is trying to matchmake with the two of us." Hazel laughed before whispering… "Or she's already guessed it isn't necessary."

"She's quite the romantic. I suspect even more so now that there is a ring on her hand." Syver ached to put his arm around Hazel's shoulder. To hold her hand as they walked to his car, to touch the woman he cared about after their long days. But he also wanted to honor her request to maintain the secrecy for a bit longer.

"Marriage brings out romance for most."

He couldn't stop the cynical chuckle as he slid into the driver's seat of his car. "Maybe, but it also brings out jealousy, anger, spite and many other emotions, too."

"You don't mean that."

He turned, stunned by the shock in her voice. "I do." Erik and his bride seemed happy enough. Their arranged marriage was doing better than Syver's mother's union.

But it was not the stuff of fairy tales.

Signe and Erik rarely spent their free time together. And she often wore the look of sadness he'd seen on his mother's face. Theirs was a royal union, not a love match.

"In my experience, marriage doesn't create the romance Meg is looking for." The memory of his mother standing outside his father's door. Tears streaming down her face.

He'd been too young to know exactly what their argument was, but he'd known his mother was hurt. Known that the cheerful face they put on for the kingdom was a lie.

"So your parents' marriage wasn't happy? Is that why family is difficult for you?" Hazel's hand lay across his knee and he put his hand over hers.

Technically, my parents weren't married.

The words hung on his tongue. Aching for a release he'd never given. The number of people who knew the truth now were just his brother and mother. The list of those who suspected but never mentioned it was considerably longer.

The one person who'd mentioned it often, though only when in the royal family's presence, was gone from the mortal realm.

"It's part of it. Royal marriages are for power, security and class. Not love."

"I see." Hazel's voice was quiet as she focused on the road.

"Luckily," he brightened, "I've no intention of having a royal marriage." He squeezed her hand.

He wasn't sure the palace would even approve

a marriage for him. A prince did not just wed in Fönn. There were agreements and controls.

Nothing like the fairy tales.

A marriage to Hazel was likely a nonstarter. The thought burned his heart. It shouldn't matter, and it never had before she'd shown up in his country.

But the thought of her never wearing his ring, even if they were together for years, cut. Far deeper than he'd expected.

Silence hung between them. Silence was a part of life. So many people felt the need to fill the quiet moments, but Hazel never had. It comforted him...usually.

Today the quiet mimicked a wall. A wall he hadn't suspected was there.

"It's been a long day." The sigh behind Hazel's words cut against his soul.

"We should take a detour." The idea bloomed, and he was already turning the car. He knew the perfect pick-me-up.

"Detour?" Hazel looked at him; he didn't glance away from the road, but his body relaxed as her hand squeezed his.

Mia's attitude, Astrid decompensating unexpectedly...

Those two things alone were a recipe for a tense day. So why was it the discussion of marriage making the car so quiet?

Asking was the right answer...but once the

question was out. You couldn't unlearn things you heard. And he wasn't ready to bridge that gap.

They'd been together for a weekend. The idea of a life without Hazel, his throat clenched before the thought even formed. He'd lived that life, and he had no intention of going back to it.

"Where's the detour?" Hazel's tone was bright.

Was she pulling away from the unexpectedly tense subject...or pulling away from him?

"The garden center." He squeezed her hand. "Your place has three plants. You can't convince me you aren't aching to add more."

She laughed, the tone off just a little. Dating your best friend let you bypass the learning curve on many things. It also meant that he knew she was pushing away feelings. Hiding hurt.

"More plants are the answer to every harsh day." She closed her eyes as she leaned her head back.

Plants were the answer today, but what happened when they weren't?

CHAPTER SEVEN

DRIFTING AROUND HER FLAT, Hazel looked at the two floating shelves Syver had helped her hang. Plants poured off each of them. In silly pots that he'd insisted on purchasing for her.

It should have been a sweet treat. A reminder that he knew her better than others. Cared about getting her something that mattered to her. But a cloud hung over the vines.

A week later and she still kept rethinking his statement on marriage. That the palace would make all the decisions. Rather than fight that, he'd just decided not to marry.

Without considering what his future partner might want.

She rolled her finger along the edge of her thumbnail, then pulled back. They'd been seeing each other for a short period. Not enough to even consider marriage.

But the idea that he'd just let the palace decide his fate. It worried her more than a lifetime of just loving each other. So much of her life had been decided for her.

Her mother's constant moves. The job with the clinic Alec had arranged. All her belongings raided by the authorities. She wasn't prepared to live a life dictated by others.

And Syver shouldn't want that either. If he accepted it, what did it mean for them?

Her throat was stuffy as she looked at the plants, worried that she was missing something important. Something that could drive everything.

Fönn's monarchy had more power than most modern monarchies. Though they had a host of advisers, the King's word was still final. An archaic rule she thought needed revised.

However, it was unlikely Syver would ever sit on the throne. And he could renounce his title, gain his complete freedom.

Freedom by renouncing who he'd been from birth.

It was an easy thought, a much harder action to take. With consequences that couldn't be undone.

Pressing her palm into her chest, she looked at the greenery, trying to see it as something other than a distraction from the tension following their marriage discussion.

Alec had used gifts that way. Bought her something when she asked questions about his work or fought over some new fancy purchase she didn't think they could afford. Redirected her thoughts with a pretty bauble. Whenever conversations started about getting engaged, or their future, or any slight argument, she could count on finding a gift on the counter.

Always something expensive. Something she didn't want.

Everyone had told her how lucky she was...of course, they'd also abandoned her after Alec's imprisonment. Gossiped over the fancy electronics and jewelry seized as evidence.

Plants weren't the same. Alec had never gotten her a plant, even though that thoughtful gift would have meant far more than any fancy electronic or jewelry she had no place to wear.

So why did the vines and silly pots give her the same uncomfortable feeling?

"Hazel." Syver swept into the flat, and grinned.

And most of her uncertainty floated away.

She was the one holding back in the relationship. She was the one who'd asked him not to discuss their relationship. Not to announce it to anyone.

Projecting her own insecurities would only hurt their future.

Still, what if she was missing something?

"I come bearing gifts!"

Gifts...

And the hint of uneasiness tripped through her as she stepped out of the small kitchen. "I don't need a gift, Syver."

"Well, the Queen will be sad to hear that." He held up a pink-and-blue box with the fanciest ribbon she'd ever seen tied on the top.

"Queen?" Hazel looked at the box, trying to figure out what the Queen of Fönn would send her. "Why would she send something to me?"

Hazel eyed the box. Syver hadn't had to tell his

family about their relationship. He wasn't technically living at her place, but he had a few changes of clothes here, a toothbrush and shampoo.

He'd told her more than once that he liked her flat better than the palace. Something she didn't believe the first time, but he'd seemed so sincere and happy when he was here.

It was only a matter of time before the staff at the hospital learned what Meg was nearly certain of. She and Syver were together.

"Gift might not be the best word. It's more invitation." Syver grinned as he set it on the table. He was nearly bouncing.

"You know what this is?"

"I do." He raised his hands and for a moment she thought he'd clap, but he spun the box so the bow was facing her.

"There is a function Queen Signe would like you to attend. She requested you."

His happiness was infectious. Hazel smiled as she looked at the pretty package. An invitation… from the Queen. That excited Syver.

"You want us to attend?"

"I very much do."

"A function with the royal family. If we attend, then I'm officially your…" Her mouth froze. She wanted to say girlfriend. It felt like that, but they'd never actually labeled this.

"My girlfriend. Yes. If you attend, our connection will be official. Meg will feel quite justified.

But if you're not ready, I can pass along your apologies."

His face fell a little on the words. He'd do it, but he didn't want to. He was excited for her to attend.

That settled the last of her nerves. "What function are we attending?"

"Open it and you'll see." Syver bounced and tapped the box again. The happiness he wore lifted away most of the worry she had about stepping out of line or doing something that embarrassed him.

A gift from the Queen. That was a plot twist Hazel from six months ago would not have believed. "I take it your brother and sister-in-law approve at least a little of you spending time with me?"

In any other relationship she wouldn't have worried over it, but particularly after Lady Penve's reaction last week, she'd been more aware of the status others would know she didn't have.

"They seem happy enough." His voice was soft, and he didn't look at her.

Hazel tilted her head. "Why does that surprise you?"

"We already know each other's little tells, don't we?" Syver's lips brushed hers.

He was trying to distract her. And kisses were the way to do it, but she would not let this go. "We do. And you're avoiding the question." Hazel crossed her arms, creating a bit of a barrier from the advances she craved.

"Most people would focus on the fancy invitation from the palace."

"You're more important than an invitation or anything else from the palace." A look passed over his face and she hated the surprise she saw there. "Syver." Running a hand over his chest, she lifted on her toes and pressed a kiss to his lips.

His arms wrapped around her waist and, like it had every other time they'd kissed, the world slowed. His lips, soft and warm, wrapped her in a protective bubble. Nothing could hurt them in this moment.

"Why does an invitation for your girlfriend surprise you?" What wasn't he saying? There was something he never said. Something he was hiding.

I'm hiding something, too.

She hadn't found a way to tell him about Alec. He knew the relationship was bad...but not how bad.

Holding her, he put his head on hers. "We were not close growing up. Erik was the heir and I..."

The hesitation surprised her. He'd been the spare. It was a word anyone who followed royal families around the globe knew. A hurtful descriptor that was still part of the everyday lexicon.

"The extra special additional bouncy boy?" She strengthened her grip on him. He was the furthest thing from the spare in her mind.

Syver chuckled. "That is a better phrasing than *spare*."

"Agreed!"

"Anyway, his training, the roles he took on, looked different from mine. He asked me to come home, but I haven't received the roles I expected. My mother and I are closer than when I was in London, but I'm left out more than included. My recommendations..." his voice trailed off.

"You're still uncertain of your place here?" That surprised her. He'd returned to Fönn over five years ago. At the request of the King.

"I am." Syver pulled back but grabbed her hand and tapped the box. "Perhaps that isn't fair. I guess I just thought I'd be more involved."

More involved.

Two words that sank against her heart. Because it wasn't involvement she thought he craved, it was acceptance.

"But this is a big deal. A big thing." He pointed to the invitation. "Open it."

Turning her attention to the box, Hazel looked at the intricate design. It seemed like something out of a movie. "I really can't imagine what the Queen would invite me to."

It was a piece of art—how was she supposed to open this? She couldn't see any seams under the bow, any areas to start the unwrapping.

It was a weird thing to be self-conscious of. But Hazel hadn't received gifts from her mother growing up. Alec had never wrapped the things he gave to soothe over arguments.

The Christmas gifts Syver had placed under their small tree were nicely wrapped, but not fancy like this.

Untying the bow, she let out a small gasp as the box fell open and paper butterflies "flew" for a moment, then landed on the table.

"The Queen certainly knows how to design an invitation!" Hazel lifted the small card inside, then did a little dance.

"A gender reveal!" The Queen was pregnant. Hazel had an invitation to the baby shower for the heir to Fönn's throne.

"Yes." Syver took a deep breath, a bit of the excitement falling from him.

"This is a happy moment, right?" Nothing about Syver indicated he wanted the throne. But to be unseated…an identity you didn't want was still one you had. The only one he'd ever known.

"Signe has struggled to maintain pregnancies. The palace has not publicized that. Everything is going well this time, but until the little prince or princess is here, I think there will be a fog of worry and concern."

Hazel understood. One in eight known pregnancies ended in miscarriages, and if one counted the number that occurred before a pregnant person realized it, that number was likely far higher. Infertility was a struggle some were very open with and others chose not to discuss. And whichever choice a pregnant person made was the right one for them.

"The gender reveal is happening before they tell the kingdom. I think they plan to announce it the next day."

"And you're okay with the announcement?"

His eyebrows knit together as he looked at her. "Why wouldn't I be?"

"Because it will make you third in line to the throne instead of heir? That might bother some people." She waited a moment, but when he said nothing, she added, "But not you."

"Not me." He dropped a kiss on her lips. "Heir to the throne isn't a title I ever expected." He shrugged as he glanced at the invitation.

She was certain there was more to it, more words trapped in his soul, ones she wished he felt secure enough to let out.

"This will be your first royal engagement, though." He pressed his lips to her forehead.

First...

Royal marriage might be off the table, but the future wasn't. That was lovely and terrifying. What happened if she messed up?

"Are there protocols I need to follow?" His arms tightened.

Was he being protective...or worried...or both?

"Yes. But there is plenty of time to discuss those. Not what I want to do tonight."

"So what do you want?" Hazel kissed him, meaning it to be a quick peck like his kiss. Instead, his arms pulled her even closer, his mouth opened and everything but her need disappeared from the world.

"You." The word was a growl. In this room there was no prince, no aristocrat. Their tongues danced together, and he lifted her onto the counter. She wrapped her legs around him. Hugging him tightly as his mouth devoured hers.

"I know we were supposed to go to dinner." Syver muttered as he trailed a kiss along her jaw.

"We still can." It was a joke. If he tried to take her anywhere but bed, she'd throw a fit.

His fingers gripped her backside through her pants, and she couldn't stop the whimper of need on her breath.

"Really?" He nipped at her ear.

His manhood pressed against her and she knew a tease when she heard it. Shifting her hips just slightly, she relished the groan pouring from his mouth. "You want me as bad as I want you."

His touch woke the siren in her. Her body sang for him, craved him, and right now, she had a very specific song in mind. She slipped off the counter, her fingers skimmed his hard length as her tongue danced with his.

Syver groaned, and it was music to her needy self. Her fingers undid the buttons of his pants as his hands ran over her breasts. Her nipples tightened, but she knew if he stripped her, she'd lose control.

And this moment, this moment, was about making Syver lose his.

After pushing his pants to the ground, Hazel traced her finger across his tip then slipped to her knees, loving the control she had over this moment.

Syver's hands wrapped through her curls as she kissed her way down his length, cupping him, then working her way back up with her tongue.

Her own need was smoldering as she took him fully, using her mouth to drive him toward the edge.

"Hazel…" His hips rocked, and she looked up, enjoying the pleasure enlivening his features. "Sweetheart…" His fingers stroked her chin, the urgency in his tone as he tipped fully over orgasm's cliff.

Only when she'd taken all of him did she finally rise from her knees.

"Hazel," his bright eyes stormed with desire as he started unbuttoning her shirt, his fingers tracing the inches of skin he'd uncovered. "My turn."

Such promise in two short words.

"Do I look okay?" Hazel smoothed out the light pink dress he knew she'd purchased for this party.

He hated the look of panic that she'd hidden quickly. Today was a big deal. One she couldn't fully understand.

Syver hadn't expected an invitation to this event for himself. Erik rarely invited him to gatherings, but to get an invitation for himself and Hazel. He wondered if his mother had begged her oldest to include them. Either way, it was a significant step.

Maybe Erik was finally ready to fully welcome him *and* Hazel. An acceptance he'd craved all his life, to get it with Hazel. There was no better gift.

"You're gorgeous." She'd left her curls loose, painted her full lips red, and he ached to kiss them. But if he started, he'd likely sweep her away to his room and spend the night ensuring she wore nothing but the lipstick.

And he wanted her at this party. The intimate gathering of a few trusted aristocrats, Signe's family and Security, was the perfect place to introduce Hazel. Ease her into the royal world.

His role in the family wasn't as high-profile as people assumed. The palace used his position at the hospital to argue that he was too busy for some royal obligations. A convenient excuse that kept him away from all but the few events where his absence would be noted.

When the Prince or Princess was born, he'd be able to step back even more. *Able, expected...*

Technically, it was the second of those things. But by couching it as able, it gave Syver the feeling of a little more control.

"I curtsy to the King and then the Queen, correct?"

"Yes." Pressing his lips to her forehead, he sent a silent prayer to the universe that this didn't scare her away.

He needed Hazel. And he wanted to make the

family happy. Maybe even happy enough that they'd consider granting them the right to marry.

Doing it without his family's approval... Syver couldn't imagine that. It would be a slight directly against the King. And going against his brother would lose him the little ability he had to support the health initiative. To combat the horrid ideas presented by people who'd never served in a medical setting.

Lady Penve and her like-minded cohorts would swoop in as soon as he held no power. Separating care for their children, leaving the others with what? Who would advocate for all the children of Fönn?

So Syver needed to play by the royal rules.

"And if I mess up?" Her voice wobbled just a little.

"If you mess up, I'll let you know. We all mess up at first." It was true, but Syver also planned to keep an eye out for the head of the protocol office.

If she started for Hazel, he'd run interference. Marge had controlled the office with an iron fist since before King Eirvin's reign. Or at least it felt that way. She relished correcting small slights and had recommended more than one palace ban for slights she considered large.

Erik had reined her in—but she still pushed the boundaries.

Arne, the head of Security, approached and

dipped his head. "Your Royal Highness… Ms. Simpson."

"You can call me Hazel."

Arne shook his head. "No, I can't."

Hazel looked at Syver, and he held up a hand. It wasn't worth arguing over. Arne was focused on the royal family, but not Syver. Not really.

The imposter heir got the basics. Nothing more.

"I did not run a full security profile on Ms. Simpson. Given that it was my understanding she wasn't visiting the palace. The invitation…"

Arne didn't complete the sentence, but Syver heard the words. Hazel's inclusion was a surprise, a last-minute gift from the palace.

"Security profile?" Hazel stiffened beside him.

"It's standard, sweetheart."

"It is, and typically completed before anyone has access to the royal family."

Hazel chuckled and looked at Syver. "Well, I had access to the royal family for years in London. Lived with them even."

"Prince Syver was not considered part of the household then. His security was not a priority for King Eirvin."

"Excuse me?" Hazel moved, but he caught her, holding her tightly to him.

Now it was Syver stiffening. Arne was simply relaying the truth. King Eirvin hadn't cared; getting upset didn't change anything.

Hazel wrapped her arm around his waist. "You all right?"

No. But now wasn't the time or place. "Fine." He didn't look at her, knowing she'd see the hurt Arne's words caused. She was already angry on his behalf.

If she knew the words felt like daggers ripping through him, he doubted they'd make it through the garden party. And he wanted this day to go well.

Needed it, too.

Syver's feelings rarely mattered. So he did as he always did, pushed the feelings away.

That was a skill all the royals excelled at.

Arne looked to Hazel. He could see the security officer making judgments. Which was his job but Hazel wasn't a security risk.

"If anything happens to the royal family—"

"Prince Syver is part of the royal family."

"Hazel."

"Syver?" Her eyes blazed as she looked at him. His own champion.

The words caught in his throat. No one championed him. He was the black sheep, the imposter heir. The only role he'd ever known. She was ready to fight the head of security…for him.

A role even his mother rarely took up.

"It's all right." His voice was soft. This was the role he played. His position in the family—one earned through no fault of his own.

"It's not." She lifted her hand, cupping his cheek. She turned to Arne. "But I will not put *any* member of the royal family in danger."

"Syver!" He wasn't sure whether the arrival of his mother into this maelstrom was a calming force or an agitating one. The Dowager Queen could be difficult to read, even for her son.

"You must be Hazel Simpson. The young woman who's captured so much of my son's attention."

His mother smiled at him. "She is gorgeous."

She is. Inside and out.

Hazel dipped into a curtsy. She wobbled slightly, but for a first attempt it wasn't bad.

"Come with me, dear girl." She pulled Hazel to her feet. "We have much to discuss."

Syver followed, but his mother held up her hand. "Syver," she laid her free hand on his arm, squeezing it lightly. "Erik wishes to speak to you. I'll escort Hazel into the garden."

Hazel's eyes widened as she looked back at him. His mother pulled her along, though pull was too strong of a word for the Dowager Queen's actions. But the effect was the same. "Tell me about Syver in London. He rarely talks about his time there." His mother winked, clearly happy to have found Hazel.

"I'll see you shortly," Syver called, wondering how much of their story Hazel would spill and glad that his mother had sought her out.

* * *

Hazel wasn't sure what she'd expected for the gender reveal party. It was like those she'd attended for friends in London. The decorations were all pink or blue. Cupcakes swirled with pink-and-blue icing.

But it was clear where the preference lay...and what was expected.

People were putting little blue strips into a bowl, voting for a prince. The bowl for the Princess was empty until Hazel dropped a vote in.

Syver's mother had told her that no princess had been born in the royal line for four generations. When she'd quipped that perhaps it was time then, the Dowager Queen had looked horrified. If hoping for a girl was such an issue, why have the gender reveal at all? Hazel had known enough to keep that thought to herself.

Not that she'd had many people to talk to. Syver's mother had grilled her for stories about her son. They'd laughed and seemed to be having a grand time. Until they entered the garden. Then it was like a shield had fallen in front of the woman.

The Dowager Queen, doing her duty.

She'd stayed by Hazel for a little while, then been pulled away. Queen Signe had nodded to her when Hazel said she was glowing, and the rest of the invited guests had found other places to be as soon as she wandered their way.

The snub wasn't subtle.

It's not supposed to be.

She was being put in her place. Spoiler alert, Hazel knew her place and her exclusion here didn't bother her. But would it bother Syver?

He was different inside the palace. The shift between Prince Syver and just Syver, as he liked to call himself, was on display. She wasn't sure what to make of it.

Her family wasn't loving, hadn't cared for her, so she knew what toxic relations looked like. She just hadn't expected to find them here. They'd called him home. Flown him home so quickly, reintegrated him into their home for the public eye.

Behind closed doors, though.

"You doing all right?" Syver's voice was calm as he slid his arm around her waist.

She opened her mouth, planning to say yes. To just get through this, but the word wouldn't form. "No one wants me here."

"That isn't true. I do." He grinned, but his eyes shifted, surveying the crowd.

Surveying the enemy.

And he didn't lie and say she was just reading too much into it.

"Why was I invited?" That was what she couldn't understand. They'd addressed the invitation to her. Syver had thought his brother was happy for him. Yet, it was clear that everyone wished she'd stayed home.

"I'm not sure, sweetheart. I think my mother

wanted to meet you. But out here, she's doing her duty. Like always." The line between his eyes deepened and a heaviness clung to him.

He'd been so excited for her to receive an invitation. All that joy evaporated as the reality of the day set in.

"Let's just get through the party. We're a team." He squeezed her.

"A team." Repeating the words made her feel a little better. "What did your brother want?"

"To let me know that another petition was put before him regarding a private hospital."

"Private is just another word for exclusive. I worked in one once—we turned away far too many patients. At least, in my opinion." Bitterness floated through her. She'd watched people keep her out because she'd been born to a single mum who lived just above the poverty line.

Those same people had pretended to accept her after Alec's "business" took off. Then relished his downfall, and by association, hers. It was bad enough when people wanted to keep professional and personal relations separate from those they considered less than them.

But medical services.

That was a special brand of evil.

"Did you explain to the King why that wasn't appropriate?"

"I did. And he's listening to me." There was a hint of surprise at the end of his sentence.

"Good." Hazel leaned her head against his shoulder, wishing this day was over. If she never stepped into the palace again, it wouldn't bother her.

"We're cutting the cake in five minutes. If you've not voted for prince or princess, now is the time." The staffer's call echoed across the crowd.

The palace baker had created the cake. If it was pink on the inside, then a princess was on the way, and if it was blue, then most of this party was going to be excited.

"Did you vote?"

"For a princess. You?"

"I'm not allowed to. They are doing a drawing out of the winning bowl. Royal family isn't allowed to take part. Might look bad if we won our own gift."

"Your mother voted."

"Did you see her actually drop her name in the bowl?"

Hazel started to say yes, then replayed the interaction. "I don't recall."

"It's a standard royal trick. Distract and then people think you participated without you actually doing it."

"Cake time." The staffer called and the attendees all moved as one toward the stand.

The excitement she'd witnessed at other parties was nowhere to be found. There was no squealing, no clapping, no last-minute calls for a boy or girl. It was a production, but it lacked any heart.

The King and Queen stepped to the cake and lifted the knife.

"Are they hoping for a prince or princess?" She knew the crowd wanted a prince, but surely in the twenty-first century, the royal couple would be happy with either.

"A boy. If it's a girl, well, then if the Queen has another baby and it's a boy, that will supersede his sister. So the hope is always for a boy first. My brother really wanted to do this, the first royal gender reveal. Even though everyone said it was silly since no princess has been born—"

"In four generations. At least I understand why your mother was so horrified when I said it was time for a princess."

"You didn't!" Syver let out a chuckle, then quickly controlled it. "Mother probably privately enjoyed it. Not that she would show it here."

"I didn't realize it was a misstep. My boyfriend didn't let me in on the secret."

"My apologies."

Hazel looked at the couple. They sliced the cake and she saw Queen Signe's face dip.

It's a girl. And she isn't happy.

Hazel's heart ached. If the queen's husband had pushed this reveal, a fun tradition where the ultrasound technician put the gender in an envelope to give to a baker or family member, so the expectant parents could be surprised at their party.

People recommended not doing a gender reveal if

you might be upset by the outcome. But if you'd had boys for four generations and expected a prince…

The Queen's bottom lip quivered for just a moment before she controlled the action.

"Princess!" King Erik announced.

Hazel clapped, the sound clear in the quiet. She saw a few heads turn her way, but she wouldn't act like this was a sad moment. A princess was coming. Signe was pregnant and healthy. The baby was healthy. This was a joyous moment.

She looked at Syver, and he clapped with her.

"Congrats, Signe and Erik! A little niece for me to spoil."

The rest of the crowd started clapping then.

Queen Signe's eyes found hers, and there was a softness in them that had been absent before. She nodded to Hazel.

At least this wasn't a complete failure.

CHAPTER EIGHT

"DR. BERNHARDT'S PHONE."

Syver heard Hazel's words as he opened his eyes. Light was streaming through her window. Rubbing his face, he sat up. Yesterday's garden party had exhausted him, but not hearing his phone was something that never happened.

He wasn't on call, but that didn't mean other physicians didn't ring. Consults and emergencies rarely cared about the schedule.

Work was the reason he was back in Fönn. The way he gave back to the country. The way he'd proved himself.

He slid to the side of the bed and yawned, not quite ready to start the day.

"No, I've not seen it. How would I even do that? No, he doesn't know."

The shift in her tone activated Syver's body. Something had upset Hazel.

Yesterday had been a lot. Erik had told him that he was looking forward to how Hazel did. For a moment, he'd thought the walls were falling around the royal family...for him.

Instead, it had seemed like an intentional snub. At least his mother had liked Hazel, and the Queen had softened toward her, too. Signe had sought Hazel out after the announcement that she was carrying a princess. The heir to the throne was going to be a girl for the first time in a hundred years.

And only Hazel had clapped. Even he'd stood there stunned. The expectation was a boy. A prince. Erik looked stunned as well. The Queen looked defeated. Until she'd caught Hazel's look, seen the happiness and joy in Hazel's celebration. Every bit real—not faked for the Queen's enjoyment.

The first person she'd talked to after the announcement was Hazel. Who'd reacted with warmth and excitement as Signe discussed names and nursery decorations.

The aristocrats could ice them out, but if the Queen accepted her, eventually maybe the King would, too. Then everyone else would fall in line, even if they didn't want to.

Walking into the kitchen, he held out his hand. Hazel dropped the mobile into it immediately. The color was gone from her face, and she was wiping tears off her cheek.

"Why is my girlfriend in tears?" He opened his arms, but Hazel walked into her bedroom, her head hanging and her shoulders screaming defeat.

Someone was going to pay.

"There was a leak from the garden party. *Someone* tipped the press to the Queen's pregnancy and the fact that it is a girl."

And Arne automatically assumed the someone was Hazel. Of course, the head of Security was reaching out here first. "And you think Hazel had something to do with it?"

"Given her previous association with a con man who is serving over ten years for fraud—"

"What?" The word fell out before he had time to think. The royal family could use the slip against her and him. He'd vouched for Hazel. Sworn there was nothing to find.

"Something she kept from the heir to the throne, too."

She had, but he could hardly hold that against her. He'd kept his literal identity from her when they'd lived together for years. Even now, he'd not let her in on the state secret regarding his birth.

He trusted her implicitly. Hazel wasn't the leak.

She would never announce something so important for someone else. "She didn't tip the press. I doubt she even knows how."

That wasn't something anyone discussed, but most "unplanned" photos or news releases regarding the royal family or aristocracy were planned leaks. Public relations in the digital world was an art form, but one noncelebrities rarely knew how to navigate.

"Hazel Simpson is banned from the palace." Arne's voice was tight. "As the head of Security, I will also recommend to the King that your association with her be discontinued."

Syver hung up without responding.

He didn't think Erik would order him away from

Hazel. But there were other ways to pressure him. His stomach turned on the thought. Erik could make Syver's life difficult. Could withhold money from the projects he sponsored.

He could send me away again.

The tiny voice in the back of his head sent fear ringing through him. It had felt nice to get away from Fönn when King Eirvin was in charge. But he'd missed his family, even if they weren't the picture-perfect example of love.

He didn't want to lose them. Not again. But he couldn't lose Hazel either.

"I didn't call anyone."

"I know."

She sank into the bed on those words, her shoulders collapsing as a sob left her chest. "You believe me."

"I do." Syver sat beside her and pulled her to him. Running his hand along her arm, he kissed the top of her head. He didn't want to push, but he needed to know about the con man issue.

"But I need to know about—"

"Alec was my boyfriend. I met him not long after you left. I was lonely, and he said all the right things."

Her shoulders shook, but Hazel didn't stop. "He was starting a business. In medical research, a lot of technical IT jargon. Or at least that was what he said. Maybe it was even the truth at the beginning. That was his defense at trial. But the reality is I don't know."

Syver said nothing. He didn't quite understand what she was saying.

"We lived together for two years. I told you it was bad, but I thought, well, I thought it would get better, or I hoped it would. And the business, it wasn't real. All fraudulent investments, robbing Peter to pay Paul."

She blew out a breath. "He helped me get a job at one of the private clinics 'funding' his tech. Nursing manager at a high-end pediatric clinic, all private patients. I liked it. No, I loved it."

She ran a finger over her thumb, and he grabbed her hand before she could pull at the skin. She was hurting, but she didn't need to hurt.

"I was good at it. Managing care, ensuring the patients got what they needed, and I could bring in pro bono patients, too. I felt fulfilled in my career."

Her being good at something was the least surprising thing he'd heard. "Of course you were good at it. You're an excellent nurse."

"Alec's tech, the stuff he claimed would revolutionize patient care…a figment of his imagination and greed. Everything came crashing down a little over a year ago. The police raided our flat. All the fancy things he'd purchased were confiscated to recoup damages."

"Hazel…"

"The worst was no one believed I didn't know. Everyone thought he was so charming before the arrest. Thought the presents and the attention were perfection, never mind that my dreams were materializing. A settled life, a place that was really ours, not a rented flat, a family. A person who didn't belittle me. All of it kept slipping further and further away."

She laughed, but there was no humor in it. "He was perfect...until the raid. Suddenly, they'd all suspected something. Seen a glint in his eye or heard the way he talked about something and just *known* something was off."

"And they believed you knew." He squeezed her tightly; if there was a way for him to wipe away the pain, or take it on, he would. He cared for her, was falling fast for her.

Hell, who was he trying to kid? He loved her. Maybe he had for years, or it had just happened fast. Either way, the truth was there. He loved Hazel Simpson. And this was the absolutely worst time to mention it.

"How does one live with a prince and a con man without knowing? Either you're incredibly naive or a liar." Her tone shifted, and he knew she was mimicking the words she'd clearly heard more than once.

"Hazel."

"And I was naive." She stood, wrapping her arms around herself. "That is something I hate to admit to myself, but it's so clear. I lived with a prince for two years and never suspected."

"Hey—"

She kept pacing, ignoring his interjection. "I dated a con man for years. Lived with him for two. I accepted his gifts, thanked him for helping me get a job. It frustrated me that he stopped talking about our future. But I never guessed. I missed all the signs. I didn't know or suspect…"

"Why would you?" He wasn't even sure she was hearing him.

"And I was naive to think it was possible I could just restart, leave Alec and the past behind. It always finds you. No one remembers the good stuff…but the bad. That will haunt you forever, even if you did nothing wrong."

"You are not naive." Syver stepped in front of her. She bumped into his chest, and he wrapped his arms around her. Holding her in place, taking in the sobs and just letting her be as she needed to be…with him. "You are kind, trusting—"

"All things that he used to take advantage of me."

The bitterness in those words. That way of thinking was damaging. And it wasn't true.

"Someone taking advantage of you says more about them than it does you, Hazel." Running his hands over her back, he held her while she sobbed and waited for her to gain some control.

"Kindness, empathy, trusting others makes you an excellent nurse and a good person. Qualities that I wish I had at the same levels as you."

"You are kind." She sniffed.

"If you could be in my brain right now, you wouldn't think so." Alec was out of his reach.

She pulled out of his arms, sniffed again and wiped her nose with the back of her hand. "I must look a real fright."

"You're gorgeous."

Hazel raised her brow. "Come on, Syver. I have puffy eyes…my nose is runny from tears…"

"You are gorgeous," he repeated, and reached for her hand. "Puffy eyes and runny nose included. You are gorgeous, period."

"At least you know all my secrets now. No more skeletons hiding in my closet."

The words hit him, and he let out a breath. She'd told him everything. All the sins that weren't hers but still weighed against her soul. And he still had a giant one.

"I'm not King Eirvin's son." The words were out. The state secret he technically couldn't tell anyone. The imposter heir and the truth behind why he'd been sent away.

And even after his recall…they didn't treat him as an equal. People assumed it was because he was at the hospital so often. Assumed those duties kept him too busy to be at the opening ceremony of Summer Nights, or state visits, or any other number of things that would normally be expected of a proper heir to the throne.

"Hazel…"

"I know."

Two little words. Two little words and a smile. His ears buzzed, his brain rattled, and now it was his turn to fall into the bed.

Hazel wasn't sure what reaction Syver had expected to his announcement, but it obviously wasn't her admitting that she knew. The truth wasn't as surprising as she was sure he thought it was.

He didn't have the traditional *E* name. All the girls' names Signe had discussed with her were *E*, and when Hazel commented on it, she'd said it was the tradition for royals.

That all members of the family had an *E* name. The tradition went back for more than a hundred years. She'd said it with such grace, such certainty. Like she'd forgotten that Hazel was dating a royal… who did not have an *E* name.

Her reaction when Hazel pointed it out, the color tinting Signe's cheeks as she made an excuse that made no sense, raised several questions. Ones Hazel didn't know the Queen well enough to ask.

Then there was Arne's statement that Syver wasn't considered part of the royal family when she lived with him in London. That he was there at all, blending in, acting like he wasn't a royal. None of that added up to a son King Eirvin was proud to have carry his name.

His birth, the scandal it must have caused, none of it mattered to her, but it clearly did to him.

"You're still Prince Syver." His mother had

had an affair, but he was still a royal. Some might whisper about his bloodline, but those whispers shouldn't matter.

Shouldn't.

Who was she to talk? Hazel had fled London to avoid whispers. And nearly collapsed in a heap on her kitchen floor when she'd heard Arne's accusations. Whispers did damage.

"Am I?"

"Do you want to be?"

Syver opened his mouth, closed it, then opened it again. But still no words came out.

"You weren't Prince Syver in London. And you mention that inside these walls you're just Syver. You seem to crave it. Do you even want to be a prince?" She doubted anyone had ever asked his preference. By the circumstances of his birth, he was royal...and not, at the same time.

But what did Syver want?

"I want my family to want me. All of me— without reservation." The words were so soft that she knew he didn't mean to speak them. And they broke her heart.

Because she didn't know if that was possible. It had taken her a lifetime and a solid therapist to understand that her mother wasn't capable of accepting her. Alec had used her, his love as fictitious as the company he'd used to scam people.

Syver couldn't control what others thought of him. Only how he reacted to their actions.

Sliding into his lap, she put her hands on either side of his face. "All you can be is your best self."

"That's never been enough."

Leaning her head against his, she held him as the sad words washed over them. He should be enough. The man was kind, intelligent, well-spoken. And none of it should matter, because as the Queen's son, the King's brother, they should love him just for that.

His pain ricocheted through Hazel's soul. His hurt, and her inability to pull it from him. If she possessed one wish, she'd use it to make him feel how he made her feel.

Whole.

Since the moment she'd seen him, her heart seemed to beat with his, her eyes looked for him. They'd been friends in London, but if he'd stayed... if he'd stayed, this would have happened.

Maybe even the night he left. All the signs were there for everyone but them to see. He was her person. The man who made her feel all the things she'd read in the romance novels she devoured.

"I love you." Maybe this wasn't the right time but waiting for some perfect moment wasn't her style. "I love you, Syver. You are enough."

Her body was lighter; speaking truth did that. She loved him. His lips skimmed hers, as his hands firm against her back pulled her even closer.

"I love you, too."

She laughed. It wasn't funny, but her body released the sound. "Syver, it feels like we have always known this. We're hopeless."

"I know. But there is no one else in the world I'd rather be hopeless with."

"How romantic!" She pushed on his shoulder before dipping her lips to his again. Movies, books, the world made a big deal out of these moments.

Videos went viral on social media with people telling others they loved them. This was such a small moment, and she wouldn't change a thing.

He held her as they kissed, enjoying each other. There was passion, but it was subdued by the morning's heavy topics.

She wrapped her legs around his waist, then leaned her head against his shoulder. Holding him as tightly as possible. "I love you."

His fingers caressed her back. "You already said that. Though I can't imagine I'll ever tire of hearing the words." His lips grazed her temple.

"Now what?" She hated to interrupt this moment, but life moved forward. If the King or Queen believed she'd leaked information, it would make life difficult for Syver.

He wanted a relationship with his family, but she wasn't willing to give him up either.

"We go to the palace."

Her blood chilled, and she knew he felt her stiffen. Maybe it was the right choice, but it was hard to catch her breath. "I'm not allowed on the grounds."

It was the second thing the head of Security said at her this morning. And he'd been very serious.

"I was told the same."

If he was nervous, his tone didn't suggest it. Was that a princely cover…or something he'd learned because he was unwanted? A way to blend in even when the world felt like it was ripping apart?

"So…"

Maybe there was some secret entrance. Some way past that only royalty knew. Arne wouldn't appreciate Syver showing her any secret entrances.

"We call his bluff."

She knew her mouth was open and her eyes must be fully bugged out. "Bluff? Syver—"

"Yep. And I think the quicker we leave, the better."

She pulled her hand across her face as she moved off his lap. "What does one wear to this type of meeting?" She was only half joking.

"Something nice."

"The nicest thing I had was the garden party dress." She wasn't planning on playing girlfriend to the Prince when she took the job on Fönn. Her closet was mostly comfy clothes, items she could change into quickly when she got off shift.

"Palace wear" wasn't filling her closet.

"Choose whatever makes you most comfortable, sweetheart. It will be okay, promise."

Promise.

She knew he meant that word, but there was a

look in his eyes. Concern…worry…fear. He wasn't sure it was going to be okay.

All right, whatever happened, they were going together. Syver and Hazel, and that was all that mattered.

Syver knew his grip on Hazel's hand was tight, but there was no way he was loosening it as they walked through the palace's family entrance.

The security person raised his head, frowned and picked up his radio. An interaction he'd had thousands of times, one that barely elicited the wave of a hand or more than a *Hello, Your Royal Highness*, was now interrupted. And he was dragging Hazel here.

He wasn't sure it was the right choice, but he also didn't know what other path to take.

"You're free to enter, Prince Syver, but Ms. Simpson—"

"Is coming with me." Syver nodded, and he kept moving. "Tell Arne that I disobeyed you. It's the truth."

No need for the young captain to get in trouble with his boss, but this was nonnegotiable, and he was making that clear now.

"Syver…"

"It's fine, sweetheart." *Man, I hope that's true.* He picked up his pace, glad Hazel followed his lead.

At least today was Sunday. The day King Erik allowed himself some rest. Until noon, King Erik and Queen Signe were in their private chambers. Up three flights of stairs, immediately to the left. He could beat Security, but it would be tight.

The King's chambers appeared, and he could hear the commotion coming down the main hall. Syver didn't bother knocking. Hopefully, Erik would forgive the intrusion.

"What—" Erik's jaw tightened as he met Syver's gaze. "She is not allowed on the grounds."

"Why? Because some article appeared, please, anyone could do that."

"Who else would have told such personal news?"

Hazel flinched, her shoulder shifting into his body.

His brother couldn't be this naive. "Many people might have shared the impending news."

"I had everyone in attendance fully vetted, except." Erik's eyes slid to Hazel.

I vetted everyone but the one you brought, Syver.

Erik didn't say it, but he didn't have to. Putting so much faith in vetting, in believing that members of the aristocracy would protect the information because of their association to the crown. It was the height of wishful thinking.

Syver would never harm his family. He'd kept secrets from the time he'd learned to talk. And he'd never fall for someone who wouldn't do the same.

The woman he loved was beyond reproach in this issue.

"Your Royal Highness," Hazel said as she pulled away from Syver just as raps started on the door.

Erik held up a hand, and Hazel stopped talking. He stepped to the door and told Security they were to wait in the hallway. It wasn't much of a win, but at least he hadn't let them through the door.

Turning back to Syver and Hazel, Erik raised his hand again. "You were saying, Ms. Simpson."

She took a deep breath, clasped her hands, then met the King's gaze. "That I didn't leak the information. You don't know me, but I swear I wouldn't share such personal information. I wouldn't even know how."

"A lot of fancy words. A quick text to a friend or a line dropped into a website tip site. It's easy."

Erik wasn't wrong. It was remarkably simple to alert people when one wanted to.

"If I wanted to out the royal family, why didn't I sell my story about Syver? Living with the Prince for two years while he acted like a regular person in London is the bigger story."

Erik's jaw twitched again, and Syver reached for Hazel's hand, but she kept going. "I am not saying your impending joy isn't big news."

"It is the heir to the crown, the true…"

He caught himself as his eyes flicked to Syver. Would the dismissal ever not sting? He didn't care about being the heir to the throne, but Erik's happiness of ensuring he was out of the line of succession, in a way that didn't mean confirming palace rumors, smarted.

"You are having a child. That the baby will wear a crown one day is not massive news." Hazel held up her own hand as Erik opened his mouth.

Silencing the King.

Syver was proud and also horrified.

"I could have had a book deal, could have done daytime talk shows. I had my chance when the crown was paying no attention and the story would have gained me something. Then it would have run on the world stage for weeks, maybe months, if I was the type of person to embellish."

She looked at Syver, her face so open. Turning, she raised her chin. "Whatever you think of me, I gain nothing from this leak."

"She's right." Signe's voice was soft, barely carrying across the room.

"Signe." Hazel didn't hesitate. She moved to the Queen's side. "How are you feeling?"

Not well.

That was obvious from the Queen's pallor.

"Faint. I can still feel the baby move, though, and I'm not bleeding."

"All right." Hazel put her arm around Signe's waist. "We are going to the couch. Can you make it that far?"

"Signe…" Erik was at his queen's side, sliding his arm on the other side of his bride.

Their marriage wasn't a love match, but Erik

cared for his wife. Signe had never stood outside these chambers begging for entrance where she should be welcomed without question.

"I gave everyone different names." She let out a heavy breath as Hazel and Erik lowered her to the couch. "The names mean it's…"

"We'll worry about that after." Hazel's words were tight.

"Afraid my wife will name you?"

Hazel didn't bother to answer the King's accusation. "Her pulse is racing, Syver."

Hurrying to the in-suite phone, Syver picked up the receiver, pushed one button and didn't wait for the palace operator to respond. "I need medic transport for the Queen from the King's chambers. Alert her ob-gyn to meet us at the hospital."

Hazel ran her hand over Signe's forehead. "She doesn't feel feverish, but she is sweating. Signe, what have you eaten this morning?"

"Nothing. I had so much at the party, I felt a little sick last night. The baby didn't seem to appreciate the fancy treats, I guess." She let out a small laugh, the sound bordering on hysterical.

Like all physicians, he'd done a rotation through obstetrics, but his knowledge was a decade old. He'd paid attention, but his rotation through pediatrics had come first, and he'd felt at home in the specialty from the first moment. So the other rotations had gotten his attention, but not his love.

"Medic here."

The door opened and two paramedics and most of Security raced in.

"I told you—"

"Not the time, Arne. Ban me from the palace after we secure the Queen." Syver kept his tone cool, as the head of Security openly glared at him. That was unusual—and he recovered quickly, wiping the expression from his face.

"Her pulse is more than a hundred beats per minute. I couldn't take her temperature, but she doesn't feel feverish. However, I noted perspiration on her brow, and she has not eaten since around..."

Hazel looked at the Queen.

"Around six last night." Signe's eyes met Hazel's, and she reached out her hand. "Thank you, Hazel."

Hazel smiled, but Syver could see the concern in her eyes. Like him, she had limited expertise in obstetrics. She knew Signe had struggled with infertility, even if she didn't know her full patient history.

They were limited in the care they could provide. And, at least for him, the ability to only provide basic care, and no reassurances, was difficult.

"Do not leave the palace grounds until I give you leave." Erik's words were stern and clearly for the security team.

Hazel waited until the King and Queen were gone before hitting Syver's hip. "Guess I'm now banned from *leaving* the grounds." Her words were bright, but he could see the frustration and concern on her face.

"Why don't I show you my wing while we wait?"

"Your wing! How fancy."

"Somehow, I thought you were joking." Hazel couldn't help her mouth falling open as Syver showed her the different rooms in his wing of the palace. "A wing, and I thought our flat in London was the height of grandeur. It was a proper step down."

"I thought of it as a step up." Syver kissed her fingers as he led her to his suites. "Most of the rooms here are empty. I have an office, which I never use, my bedroom suites and a library. Otherwise, the guest rooms are available for palace functions and such."

"It's almost like you have your own not so little flat back here." It had taken nearly twenty minutes to walk from the King's suites to Syver's rooms. And it was clear from the decor changes and lack of ornamentation that only Syver used this wing.

"I think King Eirvin preferred me as far away as possible."

"You lived down here as a child?" That horrified her. It was one thing for an adult, always in the public eye, to choose to step out of it in the privacy of their own place. But for a child to be banished in their own home.

"Syver." She reached for his hand, hating how similar their upbringings had been. Her mother hadn't had the option of sending her twenty minutes up the road to live. But if she had, she'd have exercised it at first chance.

"I got free run of the place down here, and mother visited every evening. Read me books and such."

Righteous anger stormed through her belly as those words echoed in the empty hallway.

Visited.

One did not visit their child in the spare wing of a palace.

"Ever thought of leaving? Getting your own flat in the city, nearer the hospital?"

"Hazel, are you asking me to move in with you?" The grin on his lips suggested he was joking, but there was a look in his eyes. One that called out to her.

She hadn't been suggesting that. Not really. They'd been dating for less than a month. One didn't move in that quickly…except he was already basically living at her place.

And they'd lived together once. Platonically.

"I mean, you can do better than my place, Syver. I have a rented bed, for heaven's sake."

"But the mattress is comfy." He pulled her into his arms, dropped his lips to hers, then let his hand trail along her lower back. "I'm not trying to put you on the spot, Hazel."

"I know, but you didn't answer my question. Have you thought of getting your own flat? Someplace that isn't a half-mile walk from the rest of your family."

They were the wrong words. His lips fell into a frown and his hands on her waist loosened. "Syver..."

Maybe she shouldn't push, but he deserved more. And she wanted to give him that. Show him.

"No. No, since I got back from London, I've not considered leaving. My family..." He pursed his lips and she could see him trying to find words.

Words she knew would either be a lie or a hard truth.

And she wanted him to know she understood. "My mum never wanted me, and I am not saying that your family is the same, but moving out might help. Some distance..."

"If I left completely, I would lose the little access I have to Erik. Mother tries, but there are aristocrats who are intent on having control over all things. You heard Mia—if she could convince him to create a private hospital or private wing of our hospital, she would."

"And you think Erik would do that?" Hazel understood the concern, but was it realistic?

"You saw him today. He can't believe that the vetted aristocrats at the party could have leaked, when it's clear they did. He was raised with them, sees them as friends."

"And you don't?"

"I was raised with them. No one discusses the rumors of my birth, but..."

But he'd never been part of the inner circle. Not

welcome, even though his title should have granted him access. It was what made him the man she loved.

However, her heart ached at the reality he'd experienced. And it hurt for the acceptance he was seeking. Acceptance she didn't think his family could fully give.

"I think you should move in with me." She hadn't really thought through the words, but if he was officially at her place, maybe he could see that he deserved more than the crumbs his family offered.

He deserved the world.

"Hazel…"

"I'm serious, Syver. Maybe it's a wild idea, but we've lived together before. We're excellent at it. My flat is smaller than our London place, but…" She grinned as she reached her arms around his neck, "We only need the one bed this time."

"Hazel."

"Don't think about it. Just jump with me. We can pack while we're hostages! Syver, you're already there all the time. This is just pulling your clothes and the few personal items you might like. I don't have room for the library, but for our next flat…"

"Our next flat." Syver's thumb ran across her jaw, and he brushed his lips against hers. "I like the sound of this, Hazel, of being with you."

"I love you, roomie. Now point me toward your suitcase!" She was serious. As soon as King Erik released them, they were out…period!

CHAPTER NINE

"The kitchen smells wonderful."

Hazel grinned as she lifted the crepe from the griddle. Their first Saturday as live-in boyfriend and girlfriend and she was resurrecting their old tradition.

And not getting sidetracked by the bedroom. At least not for a little while.

Syver wrapped his arms around her waist and pressed a kiss against the back of her neck. "I used to love waking up and smelling the cinnamon on Saturday mornings. I looked forward to it all week."

Lifting her head, she kissed his cheek. "I loved it, too. The first crepe I had was in the university cafeteria."

"Really?" Syver pulled back and moved to the coffeepot. "Your mum never made one?"

The mention of her mother sent the same stab through her heart as it always did. She'd cut the woman off after Alec's arrest. Not that her mother had noticed for almost a year, when she called asking for a loan, telling Hazel in crude terms that she must have hidden something away when she was sleeping with the con man. She didn't believe her when she said no, and Hazel had finally snapped. She had informed her then that she had no interest in a relationship.

Which was only partly true. She wanted a relationship. One that was loving and meant for her and her alone. But her mother wasn't willing to offer that. That didn't mean that she didn't wish the phone might ring one day with an apology, a genuine apology, and an offer to start over.

However, Hazel was wise enough now to realize that was unlikely. Maybe even impossible.

"Mum was not exactly a cook-a-morning-break-fast type of mum." Or a cook-or-care-for-you-at-all mother. She'd kept a roof over Hazel's head, but that was about it.

He'd asked after her family several times this week. She knew it was because he was missing his. She couldn't fix that for him.

His mother had called each night. A quick call, never lasting long but at least it let him know he wasn't forgotten completely. His brother had not reached out at all. He deserved more than a quick call. They should miss him. Want to know why he was gone. Beg for him to come back.

But she also knew that just because family should do something didn't mean they actually would.

"You always talk about her in the past tense."

Hazel flipped the sides of the crepe, then put it on the plate she'd laid out. "Here you go." She spun the batter, then dropped it on the griddle.

"Sorry, Hazel. I guess I just have family on the mind right now."

Letting out a deep breath, she looked over her

shoulder. Syver's neck was slumped. His eyes were tightly closed. She understood; she really did.

This was a process, and it was one she could help him with. Support him each step of the way. But she couldn't walk the path for him. Only he could do that.

If he wanted to. If he didn't, then he was in for a lifetime of pain.

"I cut my mother off. I haven't spoken to her in a year."

"You just cut her out of your life? She's family." He pursed his lips as he looked at the crepe.

Family.

A word that brought some people comfort. All it had ever brought Hazel was pain.

"Sharing DNA does not make a family." He was in the same spot. Surely he saw that?

"I spent my life trying to be the perfect daughter, trying to earn my place in her life, then trying to earn my place in Alec's. I'm not doing that anymore. I like who I am. I don't need to earn my place. Maybe I still falter with that sometimes, but I know my worth."

And you should know yours, too.

Those words were trapped in her head. She couldn't force them out. He was always going to be the imposter heir. That wasn't fair. But he couldn't change it. It didn't make him unworthy, though.

"Do you think your mother could do anything to earn your trust?"

"No." One syllable, two letters, and a world of

pain behind them. She could hope, but realism was best here. If her mother ever decided she loved her, for her, Hazel would weep with joy. That was almost as unlikely as the moon shifting places with the sun.

She knew that…now.

Putting her crepe on her plate, Hazel turned, her knees nearly buckling as his horror ran through her.

"She isn't good for me, Syver."

"I just can't imagine giving up."

"I couldn't imagine it either. Until it happened. The break was sudden. I mean, a long time coming. So long. But then one day, it was just severed. I can't explain that. In the moment, it was pain, and freedom, spun together in a horrid mixture that will be with me forever."

Syver ran a hand over his brow, then held up his crepe. "It's crepe morning. Happy times, together."

He moved to the table and she followed.

"So, I was thinking, maybe we put up a few more shelves. I know you're aching for more plants."

It was a unique way to change the subject. An offer for more plants, a treat after an uncomfortable conversation. Hazel took a sip of her coffee, then reached her hand across the table. "I'd love a few more shelves, but…"

"But—" Syver raised a brow. "Never thought I'd hear you say *but* when a plant was involved."

"Syver, I don't need a gift after each hard talk. You can ask me any question you want about my mum. I know moving out…"

"I'm not cutting my family off."

What if they cut you off? Could he live with that? Would he choose her, if they made him choose?

"And I am not saying you have to. What was right for me doesn't have to be right for you."

"I know."

Do you?

The words were on the tip of her tongue, but she couldn't bring herself to say them. This morning had been heavy enough. "As much as I want a few more plants, I wonder if it might be better to look for a new place. Somewhere a little bigger."

Syver blinked. Clearly, that was not something he'd considered. Her place was nice, but with his stuff from the palace, it was overstuffed. They didn't need a giant location, but something a little bigger, where they weren't always bumping into each other.

Though she didn't really mind bumping into him.

"Just something to think about."

"Yep. But in the meantime, plant store today?"

"Sure." Hazel raised her coffee mug, hoping it hid the downturn of her lips. She wanted him happy, but if his family never came around, could he be happy with just her?

Was Hazel a big enough gain compared to the loss of the royal family?

His phone buzzed, but Syver knew it wasn't his family. The constant rings and buzzes were from colleagues and friends, all asking the same question. Had he seen the poll?

All equally disappointed when the answer came back no, that he'd been on shift. That he'd look at the links they sent when he got home.

Home. A smile twitched across his face. Hazel's place, their place, was small, but it was home. Though she'd brought up looking for a new place a few times.

He wanted to say yes. Needed to, but part of him kept hoping his brother might reach out. Hoping his mother's short calls might turn into a visit.

The palace was only one of the residences the royal family owned. He hoped that after the initial sting of his departure evaporated, they'd ask if he'd like one of the flats or country homes.

Some indicator they wanted him close.

He'd thought of reaching out, even drafted a text then worried that the method was too little. He'd written a letter…one that was still sitting on the counter in an unaddressed envelope.

It felt more personal than an email. He could call. His mother asked each night if he was sure of the path he was taking.

And each night he lied. Said he was. But it wasn't true. Not really. He'd second-guessed himself repeatedly. However, in Hazel's presence, most of the worries slipped away.

She was his person. He knew that deep down. The one he'd looked for without knowing it. She was the strongest person he knew.

Strong enough to cut her mother off. That made a person strong. Strong. He kept repeating the word, forcing himself to choose it over the other that rattled in his brain.

Heartless.

He hated thinking that. Hated that he couldn't stop the words from appearing. Hazel was the furthest thing from heartless.

Yet, he knew she wanted him to do the same. She wouldn't say it, not yet anyway. That didn't mean he didn't see the look in her eye.

But how did one cut off one's family? How did one walk away from them? He'd done everything asked of him. Maybe he was still an outsider, but it wasn't as bad as it had been under King Eirvin.

If Hazel could see the difference…see how much better life was with his brother and mother. Maybe it wasn't perfect. But what family was?

Pulling into the small parking facility for their apartment, he smiled, pushing away the uncertainties. He was steps away from the woman he loved. He needed a shower, and he'd do his best to get her to shower with him.

"Tell me you have looked at the poll." Hazel laughed as he stepped through the door. "My phone has been ringing off the hook. And I keep having to tell people, I don't know."

"I haven't. I've gotten texts and voice mails all day, but I do not know what poll it is and why people think I should see it."

"The paper did a poll on who the favorite royal was." She looked at him with such an expectation.

He wasn't sure what reaction she was waiting for.

"Oh." Syver laughed. "Yeah, they do that every couple of years. An online thing. Not super scientific but fun for the kingdom. The King and Queen are always the favorite."

He couldn't remember a time when that wasn't true. It made sense; Erik and Signe were the ones people associated with the crown. Of course, they'd be the top answer.

Hazel's eyes widened. "Syver, you're the most popular."

He squinted, trying to see if she was pulling his leg, then he smiled. Always nice to win something. "How fun. Surprising, but fun."

Was this really what people had called him over? A poll run on a website for clicks? Either way, it didn't matter. Nothing to worry over or get too excited about.

Next year, or whenever they ran it again, it would be Erik, or maybe the new Princess.

"It's not close, Syver." Hazel's words were soft, but he could hear the concern in them.

Why would that bother her?

"Really?" He shrugged as he kissed the top of her head. "Want to shower with me?"

"Syver?"

"Hazel?" He ran his fingers along her collarbone,

just the way she liked. It had been a long day. He needed a shower, but he wanted her with him.

"You are the most popular. You don't think the palace will notice? Your brother?"

His mood took a hit, and he stepped back. "If he does, I'm sure it will be a minor discussion point. They talk about the polls every so often. However, no one makes a big deal of them."

"How many of those 'not a big deal' polls did *you* win?"

He didn't like the bite in her tone. This wasn't a big deal. He doubted Erik did more than grumble over it. "None." Syver's phone buzzed again. He pulled it out of his pocket. "It's just a silly poll."

If it made his brother notice him…made him reach out… No, he would not travel that thought pattern. This was just another day. And what he wanted was the woman before him.

"If you say so." Hazel's grin was forced as she reached for his hands. "I guess your friends, colleagues and girlfriend are just excited for you."

"That is nice." He meant it, too. It was sweet that people thought the poll mattered. Lovely to know his friends were happy for him. But it didn't mean anything had or would change.

After running his finger along her chest, he let his thumb hover over her nipple. "So…join me in the shower?"

Her gaze caught his, and she hesitated, then let her hand dip to his pants line. "Absolutely."

CHAPTER TEN

"A LETTER ARRIVED from the palace. Do you want to read it before we head to the hospital or wait?"

Her words were lead weights as she held up the envelope with the King's Seal. He wanted to rip the seal off and devour the message, throw it unread in the trash and burn it all at the same time.

The first missive to arrive in weeks. And one that was not expected.

A week after he'd moved out, Erik had sent his apologies for his accusations against Hazel. Sort of. The few words delivered by a security guard who explained that Signe had been testing her youngest sister.

A test she'd failed by revealing to the press the names she'd strategically given to her sister. Apparently, there were a handful of wrong names dancing around the aristocratic circles.

If anyone knew the real name, he thought it was Hazel. Signe had been so happy after Hazel clapped. The Queen had gravitated to Hazel following the announcement.

Since he'd moved out, Hazel had had two meetings with Signe, though Hazel referred to them only as get-togethers. Informal meetings discussing the upcoming baby and checking on Signe after the food-poisoning scare that had kept them trapped in the palace for almost six hours.

If she knew the Princess's name, Hazel was keeping it to herself until the baby was born. Even he didn't know the names Signe told her. She refused to break the Queen's trust.

It meant Hazel had earned a close confidant in the royal family...while he had lost them all. His mother still called, but she was distant, mentioning his brother and how it looked for Syver to be living in such a small place. The conversations were short.

Even his attempt to reach out to Erik about the health initiative had been rebuffed with a simple *The King is busy.*

He'd heard nothing since.

He wanted Hazel and his family.

Is that too much to ask?

It felt like his time in London—except now hundreds of miles didn't separate them. It was harder to pretend the actions didn't cut.

"Syver?" Hazel's hand was warm against his cheek. "You can do whatever you want with it. Or you can think about it while we are at the hospital. There are no wrong answers here."

Except there were. Maybe she didn't realize that. There was a wrong answer. In fact, there were several wrong answers. Answers that would make him an internal pariah. Or even more of one.

In the world he'd grown up in, he knew there was one right answer, a few half-right answers that would get ridiculed or result in small punishments, and a host of wrong answers.

"Read it for me."

Hazel pressed her lips to his. A quick kiss, a reminder that he wasn't alone.

"Brother—"

"He started it *brother*?" Erik always addressed him as Prince Syver. A formal address of titles. A reminder of who was in charge.

"He did." Hazel handed him the letter.

He barely resisted the urge to rip it from her hands. A frown passed over her features before she moved to where their bags were by the door, ready for their shift.

"He's inviting me to a family dinner. Just family..." His words drifted away.

"Family." She sighed as she slid her pack over her shoulder. "I suspect that doesn't include me."

It didn't. "I'll send along our apologies." The words were hard to say, but they were the right ones.

"No," Hazel shook her head, "you should go."

"I'm sure it's an oversight." It wasn't, and he hated the lie. Technically, they weren't married or engaged, so the family wouldn't consider her. That didn't mean he didn't consider her family.

She was, and he'd make sure they understood that at dinner. This was a onetime situation. He and Hazel came as a pair from here on out.

Hazel looked at her phone, then held it up. "We're pushing our time, Syver. We need to get moving. You haven't seen your brother or mother in weeks. Besides short phone conversations with your mother you haven't heard from them since we packed your things."

She frowned at the corner where many of his items were still in boxes.

"We need to find a new flat." Syver gestured to the boxes. The flat wasn't large enough to store his things long-term and live comfortably.

"We do." Hazel had brought it up several times. She'd even looked for a few places, nothing fancy, but a two-bedroom flat, a place that gave them a little more space.

He'd dragged his feet. Hoping for news from the palace. Hoping they'd offer them something. An olive branch…one she hadn't wanted to wait on. Now the palace was reaching out and not including her. It was time to act.

His family could doubt this relationship if they wanted. He would not let Hazel do the same. "This weekend. We will look for places this weekend."

"I'm holding you to that, Syver. Now…" She tapped her wrist.

No watch was there, but he understood the universal sign. He laid the letter gently on the table. Dinner with his family. He was having dinner with his family.

"I swear this is the third time we've been in the emergency room for something like this in the last four months."

"Sorry, Mum." The teenager looked at his mother. Tear streaks ran through the dirt on the boy's cheeks. "I really thought I had the trick down this time."

Her eyes rested on her son, and despite her frustration, Hazel could see the love radiating through the look. And the worry. "I want to support this. I do...but Niko...it's so dangerous."

"It's not, Mum. Not really." Words only a teen who still believed they were part superhuman and nothing bad would ever happen to them could utter.

"You've broken both your wrists, had more stitches than I care to remember, and now a broken ankle."

"We don't know it's broken." Niko huffed, crossed his arms, then cringed as the movement jostled his clearly broken ankle.

"It is." Syver commented as he strolled through the door. "In two separate places, I'm afraid."

He flipped the tablet around and showed Niko and his mother where the breaks were. Though it didn't take a doctor or an X-ray technician to see the lines between the bones that shouldn't be there.

"Maybe now you will reconsider this extreme biking sport." Niko's mother barely caught the sob as she looked from the tablet to her son.

"Mum. I love it." Niko's lip wobbled, and he pushed away another tear, whether from pain or worry over the sport he loved, Hazel didn't know.

The teen closed his eyes for a second, shifted,

though he was careful how he moved. When he opened his eyes, no one could miss the resolution in his features. "How long will I be in a cast, Prince Syver?"

"I don't know." Syver pulled up the swivel chair, sat and looked at the ankle. "This is a complicated break." His gaze shifted between Niko and his mother. "It requires more than just a cast."

"More how?" His mother stepped to the edge of her son's bed. "Is he going to be okay?"

"Yes, but today all I can do is splint it. You'll need to follow up with an orthopedic surgeon. I'll make the referral as soon as I splint it. They should be able to see him at the ER consult tomorrow morning or afternoon."

"Surgeon?"

Hazel grabbed the splint from the cabinet, handed it to Syver and went to stand by Niko's head. When Syver fastened the splint, it was going to hurt. He had to get the bones in the right place and secure it. Once the procedure was done, Niko would feel some relief, but there was no way to dull the initial pain of moving the bones. So Hazel would hold his arms, keep him as still as possible, so it went as fast as humanly possible.

"I'm supposed to compete in two months, Prince Syver. That's why I was trying the new trick. The tail whip is complicated, but I can do it. And if I complete it, I will definitely kick Johan off the gold medal stand."

"There are things more important than medals." Niko's mother's whisper was meant to be heard. "You are very talented, but—" She gestured to his broken bone. "This is so much to ask of yourself."

"Why can't you just support me?"

"Niko!"

"Why don't we get the splint on, Hazel?" His interjection didn't surprise her. Medical staff was often seen as background to life. Nursing school had prepped her for the injuries and diseases, but she'd not expected to be a witness to so much family drama.

"Niko, I am going to hold your arms while Dr. Bernhardt places the splint. To keep you as still as possible."

Syver nodded to her. "Niko, this is going to hurt."

"It already hurts."

Niko's mother looked to Hazel, and she could tell the woman wanted to roll her eyes. Teens were full of bravado, but their brains weren't fully formed yet, so long-term consequences were often difficult for them to imagine.

"I know." Syver's voice was patient. The exact right level of understanding and doctor authority. "But when I splint this, it's going to slide the bones back into place, and the splint will hold them there until you can get in to the orthopedic surgeon. Some describe it as fire lighting up your body. There is no way to numb it, so we go as fast as possible."

"If you need to scream, just let it out." Hazel had found that giving patients permission to let loose helped sometimes. She gripped his arms and looked at Syver.

"Ready?"

Niko's face shifted from Syver to his mother before nodding.

Syver splinted his ankle, and the scream made Hazel's ears ring. It took less than two minutes, but Hazel knew Niko would remember those two minutes for the rest of his life.

If this injury didn't make him want to stop his sport, and Hazel saw no indications that it did, then nothing would.

"We're done."

Niko let out a sob as Hazel released her grip on his arms. "I'm still going to complete the tail whip."

"Just make sure you wear a helmet."

Niko's mother's eyes widened. She opened her mouth, then shut it tight.

Syver continued, "The discharge nurse will be in with the papers shortly. And follow up with Dr. Mathias as soon as you can." Then he gestured for Hazel to follow him.

"I think his mother was hoping you'd convince him to give up the sport." Hazel kept her words low as the door closed behind them.

Syver looked at the closed door; there were thoughts running through his mind, but he didn't voice them.

"It is dangerous." She wasn't sure what the right answer was, if she was honest. She'd patched up more sports injuries through her career than just about anything else. But if a hobby made you happy, brought joy into your world, who was to argue it was wrong?

"It'd be nice if family supported the ones they were supposed to love."

A knife slid into her soul. That was commentary on his family, not Niko's. And she understood. If her mother loved her…wanted her, how different would her life be?

But would he be okay if they didn't? If he never got the support he deserved? Once more she worried that she wasn't enough. Her chest was tight; if he had to choose, would he choose her? And if he didn't, what would she do?

"Syver…"

"That sounded wrong."

Because you're speaking of you, not your patient.

"I just mean, this is clearly something that is important to Niko. That should be enough."

"And if he was an adult, I'd agree."

I want your family to support you. Want them to support us. However, I want to be first in your life. Is that too much to ask?

"But he is a child. She is trying to protect him. *That* is her role as his mother."

A role our mothers should have taken more seriously.

Hazel took a deep breath, then quietly added, "This isn't the same situation as yours."

His eyes flashed as he took a step back. "I didn't say it was."

"Syver." They were like two pieces of a whole. She knew his tells. Knew how much he wanted to be part of his family, truly part of it. Falling for her might not make that easier.

Actually, she knew for a fact it would make it more difficult. If he married, the expectation was that he'd marry a princess, or lady or heiress.

Though she figured his brother would prefer if he fell out of the public completely. And his mother seemed to let what his brother wanted go. It wasn't fair, but Syver couldn't seem to see it.

They'd called him back to Fönn because they'd needed his expertise. And the timing of today's missive coupled with the poll showing him as the most loved royal…it was suspect at best.

Deep down, Hazel thought he understood that. But accepting it…that was something different.

Loving her meant slipping further away from the royal expectations. She was not a princess or lady or anything more than a nurse. But she liked who she was. She didn't want him to have to choose, but…

In an ideal world, family loved you, flaws and all. But Syver's "flaws" weren't his.

The thing a person got the least choice over in their entire lives was the status of their birth. One did not choose their parents. Heaven knew, Hazel wouldn't have chosen her mother.

But a person got to choose as an adult who they associated with. And she feared a day was coming when Syver would have to choose, too.

What if he doesn't choose me?

Syver pulled at the collar of his shirt as he stepped into the formal dining room's entrance. Blood pounded in his ears, his heart wanted to jump out of his chest and he wished for at least the hundredth time since setting foot on the palace grounds that he had thought of a way to bring Hazel.

That would have meant standing up to his family. Choosing sides in the explosion that he'd known since he was a teenager was always hovering under the palace floors. A hum of friction that no one acknowledged but had the power to rip everything away from him.

And he wasn't ready for that.

"Your Highness." A man he recognized as part of the security team, but didn't know, offered a curt bow. "I'm Viggo. Arne's replacement."

Only a lifetime of ensuring he didn't react to bad news kept him from responding with an energetic *What?*

Arne had been with the royal family since before he was born. The man was almost an institution within the grounds. Whatever shakeup had happened in his absence must have been epic.

"Congratulations." He offered a palace smile, then stepped into the dining room. King Erik and his mother sat in their traditional places, and Queen Signe was next to his brother.

Signe sent him a soft smile, but he could see the uncertainty in her eyes. So this was an ambush. One they'd instructed him not to bring Hazel to. And like a fool, he'd listened.

"It's good to see you." His brother nodded and smiled.

Some of Syver's tension released as he met his brother's smile. Erik rarely smiled, a habit he'd picked up from his father. Smiles were treats, rewards, things he'd never earned from King Eirvin.

"It surprised me to get the invitation." May as well acknowledge the elephant in the room. Family dinner was not something the royal family traditionally did.

His brother looked at him, clearly trying to decide Syver's mood. "You left so suddenly I thought a little breathing space might be good for everyone."

"I left after you had your former head of security block my girlfriend from the palace over a lie that your queen could have easily cleared, if you'd been willing to ask."

Erik's head literally bounced back.

He hated the small joy blossoming in his belly. He'd never spoken back to King Eirvin; he'd simply agreed to move abroad. He'd even enjoyed getting away.

Meeting Hazel made all of that worth it.

With Erik, he challenged issues that impacted the hospital, children's health and a few priority projects, but as a rule, he was careful with his words and actions. He never pushed too hard. He wasn't really sure what had come over him tonight, but he was leaning into it.

"Boys." His mother offered him a smile. "You're brothers...remember. Family."

Erik didn't acknowledge their mother's statement, but it sent a small wave of comfort through him.

"Arne was so sure."

"He's always been aloof with me. For reasons I've never understood, but I suspect whatever the bias was..." Syver shrugged; whatever it was, Arne was gone.

"I loved his brother." His mother's voice was so soft, Syver wasn't sure she meant to speak.

"Your father." Her eyes shone with tears that didn't fall. "King Eirvin had him resettled abroad and he passed not long after the King. I am not sure Arne ever forgave me—but he decided to retire and your brother accepted it.

His mother's words stole the wind from Syver's lungs. The mystery of his parentage dropped so casually into the conversation.

"What was his name?" His father, at least genetically, was gone. No hope of knowing him…of finding out if he was wanted.

The room tilted and if there was air, his lungs couldn't find it.

"We aren't here to discuss the past."

"Erik—it's my father."

"A man you never knew."

Syver looked to his mother, saw her brush a tear off her cheek, then take a deep breath.

"The past is gone, Syver. Sit down." She nodded, the mask of the Queen sliding fully into place.

Duty first.

He wanted to argue, but his brain was buzzing as he fell into a chair. What was he supposed to do with information no one wanted to discuss?

"Ms. Simpson."

"Hazel." His mind might race a million miles a minute, but he would not let them other her. He knew the tricks. It was one thing to employ them against him, another to use them on Hazel.

"What are your intentions?"

"Intentions?" Repeating the phrase didn't unmuddle his mind, but it bought him time.

"Yes." Erik shook his head. "As a reminder, marriages of Fönn's royals must be approved by the crown."

Marriage.

He wanted to marry her. Wanted his ring on her finger, but he'd never believed the crown would approve a union. If there was hope…he'd do nearly anything for it.

Signe turned to look at him. There was hope in her eyes. For Hazel, for herself, for him? He wasn't sure, but it calmed his nerves.

Focus on the future. On Hazel and the family he still had.

"I love her. It's as simple and complicated as that. My future is with her. We are looking for a new flat this weekend. Hers is—"

"Too small for a prince." His mother's voice was firm. It was the same refrain she'd repeated each time she talked to him on the phone.

"Her flat is small, but that isn't the reason we are looking for something new." It was part of it, but he would not add to his mother's dismissal tone. The flat was nice, but it had rented furniture. It wasn't hers or his and she wanted something that was.

Something he should have agreed to the first time she'd asked. Though the way his brother was looking at him, the hope that he might be right, that the crown might offer them a place, seemed possible. That would solve so many things.

Wouldn't it?

"I agree. It looks," Erik tilted his head, clearly weighing his words, "off for a member of the royal family to be living in such a situation. The good news is that I have a solution."

"A solution?" Syver looked from Signe to his

mother, but neither met his gaze. The King was in charge, duty first. "Meaning?"

"Meaning I had Protocol find a location that is suitable for you and Ms.—Hazel. It is downtown, a penthouse—you can use furniture from the store-house, move your bed."

Syver blinked. It was what he'd wanted. But to hear his brother offer it. His voice was hoarse as he bent his head toward the head of the table. "Thank you."

"There will be some functions that we might want to host at your place. With," Erik paused again, "with Hazel."

"Of course." Syver nodded. His heart was close to exploding. His mother smiled, and for the first time in his memory, he felt like a member of the royal family. A full member.

He'd worried this was a meeting to convince him to give up Hazel, something he wasn't willing to do. Instead, he was getting the best of both worlds.

His family was bringing him and Hazel into the fold. If only she was here to hear it, too.

"The penthouse is ready to move into—simply let the staff know what to take out of storage. Once your place is set up, we plan to have a photography spread done, showing the modern royal family."

Pushing for modernization, away from a focus on the aristocracy and their wants, was a goal he'd nearly dropped. Now he and Hazel could do that… together.

"For the next family dinner, I'll bring Hazel."

"I'd love that." His mother reached for his hand as Erik looked away.

Erik motioned for dinner to be served, but he looked unhappy. Like this wasn't what he really wanted. A tinge of worry pierced the back of his mind, but he pushed it away. After a lifetime of trying to belong to his family, really belong, it was happening. And Hazel would be by his side, with his family's blessing.

CHAPTER ELEVEN

"WHAT DO YOU THINK?"

Hazel knew he wanted her to be excited, but as she looked out the penthouse window, her mouth refused to utter any words. A warning bell rang in her soul. She'd ignored them before...and lost everything with Alec. She didn't want to listen to them now, but her body was screaming that she didn't want to live here.

"This place is enormous." Syver exuded over-the-top energy that she couldn't replicate for him.

That was true. It was larger than any flat she'd lived in. "Is the size important to you?"

Syver's face fell as he shook his head. "Not really."

He'd learned about his father and seemed to push away the hurt that reveal caused. She'd tried to discuss it, tried to see if he wanted to broach the subject with his mother. But Syver repeated what he said Erik had said, it was the past.

It was...but an important part. And she worried the approval of his brother was overshadowing everything else.

Syver wanted to believe this was approval. Wanted this to show there was a thawing in the relationship. That the future was bright.

Maybe it was the start of something. Maybe she was just being too sensitive, but she didn't like

Syver's mention that there were expectations that the royal family would use this space for photo opportunities.

She'd asked if the royal apartments were used in such a manner. Syver had said, of course, not. Such a quick response with none of the follow-on thought of why their place would have that expectation.

No worry over why this place would be the foundation for the "modern" royal family. No thought his reputation with the people had something to do with it. That it wasn't really Syver they wanted, but the ability to leech off his goodwill.

Syver was popular. Maybe not with his family, but with the people of Fönn. She saw it every day in the hospital. When they walked around the gardens or visited the garden center. He was one of them, truly.

King Erik could not make the same claim. In fact, she'd heard more than one rumble it might be better if Fönn's monarchy had less control. That in this day and age, having a powerful king made little sense.

Something Hazel privately agreed with.

Syver held far more power than his brother… but she didn't think he realized it. *Or he doesn't want to.*

"You're picking at your thumb."

Hazel pushed her hands into her pockets. Her nail beds were healthier than they'd been in years, but there was an undercurrent of worry she couldn't quite force herself to ignore.

The same feeling she got the last time she saw her mother and when she broke up with Alec. A feeling that she was about to be cast out. She'd thrown walls around her heart when she'd felt the end coming with Alec. She hadn't expected the raid, but it was her naivete that had broken her, not her love for the con man. Her childhood had created nearly impenetrable barriers with her mother… once she'd finally announced her boundaries and stuck to them.

She had no protections with Syver.

Because I don't need them.

She wanted to believe that inner voice. Wanted to believe that this penthouse was a gift with no strings attached. That if they turned this down, life could be happy.

That there wouldn't always be the need to worry about what the palace thought.

"What if I want to keep looking?" She pursed her lips as Syver's mouth opened then closed with no words coming out.

"We found a few other places." The cottage she'd found, the one she loved, was perfect for them. It gave them privacy, a little more room. Their own place.

Something truly theirs.

"None were as nice as this, though, right?"

His challenge surprised her. Crossing her arms,

she shrugged. "I guess that depends. As nice as this is aesthetically, no, but the other ones don't come with strings attached. Which I think makes them nicer."

"That isn't fair." Now it was Syver burying his hands in his pockets.

Maybe it wasn't, but it didn't make it less true. "Syver, we don't have to choose this place. Can we at least look at some others? Maybe you'll fall in love with one of them."

He bit his bottom lip and looked around the penthouse. "I'm not sure Erik will understand if we pick another place. I don't..."

She waited for him to finish the sentence, but when he didn't, she guessed at the end. "You don't want to make him angry."

"I've never been asked to do anything other than help rebuild the medical infrastructure. And even my participation in that is limited to the crumbs he gives me."

"And you've done a fantastic job, even with the crumbs, as you say."

What would happen if he just stepped out as Syver, no title to his name? People without titles worked on important causes all the time. He could make even more of a difference. He could.

"The children's hospital will one day be one of the best in the world. I do not doubt that." His work in the medical field was an impressive accomplishment, one he'd earned on his own!

"For once, I feel like it's possible for me to be part of the family. I got invited to dinner, and he's offering this and hosting events here."

"What happens if you upset him? Or I do?"

Syver reached for her hands, and she let him take them, needing the connection. They were so close to a fight, one she didn't want to have, but feared might be inevitable.

"We aren't going to upset him."

That didn't answer her question.

"What if we do? What is the punishment? Is it banishment?" She laughed, but the sound died in her throat as she looked at him.

"Syver…"

"A prince needs permission to marry."

"Only if he wants a royal wedding." She remembered the words, too. And she wanted to marry him, wanted him by her side forever. But she didn't need or want a royal wedding.

But getting married without permission would cut him off forever. Her heart clenched. So they'd lived together forever, if necessary. She'd made peace with that already. She loved him. A marriage certificate didn't change that.

"We've been together for less than two months. We can worry after marriage agreements and permissions in a year or so."

"Hazel—"

"Syver." She couldn't stop the interruption. This flat was beautiful. Made for the camera, even, but she couldn't agree to it. At least not right away. "Can we just look at a few other places? Please." If they took this option, they'd live in grandeur. But the consequences...they might not survive them.

"Hazel showed me the cabin you were looking at yesterday. If you don't snap it up, Laura and I might swoop in." Dr. Lindgren, the pediatric cardiologist, grinned as he passed Syver some paperwork to sign.

Syver made a noncommittal noise. He knew exactly which place Dr. Lindgren was talking about. A small place, at least compared to the penthouse his brother was offering. The cabin overlooked the sea. It had a greenhouse, and three bedrooms that were warmed by the sun. It was all wood and felt like walking into a faery cottage.

It fit Hazel perfectly. She loved it, but it wasn't the penthouse. Choosing it would be seen as a direct statement against Erik. Maybe that wasn't fair. It was their home, but Syver had played this game his entire life. He understood the rules.

Choosing the cottage would cut his ties to the royal family. The only family he had left.

Maybe forever. He wasn't ready for that.

Moving out was the correct choice. Hazel was right about that. The penthouse was a gift; sure there were strings attached to it. That was life in the royal family, and it wasn't like his family was the only one that attached strings to things.

It was human nature.

"Hazel loves it."

Dr. Lindgren laughed. "Can I give you some free advice from a man that's been married for almost three decades?"

He didn't wait for Syver's approval. "If it makes the woman you love happy, it's the right choice. I would be happy in a hole in the ground if that was what Laura chose."

"Even if it meant angering your family." He hadn't meant for those words to escape his soul.

Dr. Lindgren looked at him, really looked at him, and Syver had a difficult time not shuffling his feet as the older man's eyes took him in.

"Family is important."

Exactly.

Before Syver could agree, Dr. Lindgren added, "But family is what you make it. It doesn't always include those that society says it should. Love is worth risking it all."

It was a nice thought, but life was more complicated than that. His mother hadn't chosen romantic love. His father, a man gone before Syver even knew he'd existed, loved his mother. And she'd chosen duty. The royal family. That was a form of love, too.

Dr. Lindgren looked at his wrist, took in the time and raised a hand. "Laura's expecting me for dinner. Good night, Dr. Bernhardt."

"Night." He turned and saw Hazel walking up the hallway.

Her quick steps and the deep worry line on her forehead set off warning bells in his brain. He loved her, but he could see the fires of concern in her mind, too. The little tells that often took months, or even years, for partners to recognize, were visible to each of them even though they'd been together less than two months.

"We've got a sixteen-year-old in Room Three. Lars is presenting with anemia and has a history of acute lymphoblastic leukemia. He's been in remission nine years."

Syver blew out a breath. Acute lymphoblastic leukemia, commonly called ALL, was considered the most survivable childhood cancer. It had a five-year survival rate of over ninety percent.

But cancer, no matter the survival rate, was always terrifying.

"Who is his oncologist?"

"Said the doctor emigrated seven years ago. He'd been in remission for three years then, his mother should have gotten another, but…"

Hazel shrugged and looked at the floor. It was a story they heard all too often, should have followed up, meant to follow up, then life got in the way. It seemed fine until it didn't.

"He's scared."

"I bet." Syver took a deep breath. There was little they could do in the emergency room. The point of the place was stabilization and moving on, and the terror seeping through the teen's veins, only hearing the words *cancer-free* could clear that.

Words Syver could not utter.

"All right, let me check him and we'll see if he needs to stay for observation or if I can discharge him to see Dr. Holm."

"Meg already texted her. I guess they worked at the same place in Maine. When Dr. Holm returned home, she convinced Meg to come, too."

Syver nodded as he took in the information in Lars's chart. He was tired, had some aches in his bones and was anemic. All symptoms he presented with when he had cancer the first time.

However, those symptoms didn't mean his cancer had returned. The aches and tiredness were symptoms of anemia. A diagnosis with a range of causes.

"Before you go in…" Hazel hesitated, looked to the room then back at Syver, "There is some family drama. Not sure what kind, but the mum's been on the phone. Some heated words and tears were exchanged."

It wasn't an uncommon theme. Emergencies brought out a range of emotions, even in families that weren't experiencing any other crisis moments. And more families than people wanted to admit were in the middle of a crisis.

"Thanks for the heads-up." Syver raised his hand. ".Shall we?"

Hazel fell into step beside him and, even with the ripple of tension between them, Syver's spirit raised. He and Hazel together. This was his happy place.

"Good evening, Lars. I'm—"

"Prince Syver." Lars smiled, though it wasn't bright. "I've always wanted to meet you. Though not this way."

Syver reached out a hand, and Lars shook it. "I'd rather our greeting was in another location, too. Where is your mum?"

"Fighting with my aunt...like usual." Lars's cheeks colored, and he looked at the floor. "They own a bakery, inherited after my nan passed a few years ago. They are always arguing about the direction of the place."

Syver looked at the door, then cleared his throat. Fighting with your sister while your son was in hospital was not a choice he'd make, but his focus was on Lars.

"I'll see if I can track her down." Hazel headed back through the door.

"What's the palace like?" Lars's feet kicked the air as Syver pulled his stethoscope from his pocket.

Lonely was the most accurate description, but not what people wanted to hear. "Busy. There is always something going on." Which was also true.

"But we aren't here to talk about the palace." Syver kept his voice light, but Lars still grimaced.

"Nope. We're here to talk cancer." He laughed, but it quickly turned into a sob.

"We're here because of your anemia, which can happen without a reemergence of your cancer." It was possible his cancer was back, more possible than Syver wanted to admit, given his medical history. But it could be something else causing it, too.

"Tell me your symptoms."

Holding up his fingers, Lars started ticking off, "One, I'm tired. Two, I'm pale. Three, my stomach hurts after I eat."

"Wait, your stomach hurts?"

"Yeah. It started a few weeks ago—before that I figured the tiredness was because I was studying for exams. I want to be a doctor, which means I need high marks for university. I remember the stomach pains from last time. I'd eat something and I couldn't keep it down. I lost so much weight."

"But you were on chemo?"

"Right." Lars sighed. "Not looking forward to that again."

Lars didn't understand what Syver was saying, but that was all right. If he was right, the cause for the anemia, while serious, likely wasn't a cancer recurrence.

"Do you eat tuna or salmon?" He knew he was on the right track by the grimace passing over Lars's features.

"Not anymore. An hour or so after I eat them—'

"Your stomach burns."

"Yeah." Lars blinked and leaned back in the observation chair. "How did you know?"

"Medical school." Syver winked and then requested a gastric consult for Lars. "If I'm right, you still need to see Dr. Holm, our oncologist, to get back on your annual checkup schedule, but you also need to see our gastroenterologist. The anemia could be because of a peptic ulcer."

"Found your mum." Hazel's cheeks were red, and she was having a bit of trouble catching her breath. "She'll be in shortly."

Had she chased the woman down?

"Good." Syver turned his attention back to Lars. "I'm going to chat with your mother until you see the gastroenterologist. She'll need to adjust your diet. No fatty foods, and you need to make a list of any foods that trigger the pain. The anemia is likely because the ulcer is bleeding."

"It's weird to be happy about that." Lars covered his mouth with his hand and his shoulders shook. "I've been prepping…and…"

"And worrying. That is completely normal." Hazel stepped to the side of the observation chair and patted Lars's shoulder.

Syver made eye contact with her, and she nodded. She'd stay with Lars while he talked to the mother.

Stepping into the hall, he nearly bumped into a tiny dark-haired woman who was furiously typing away on her phone.

"Excuse me," Syver started, but she waved a hand at him. He waited a moment, then cleared his throat. "Are you Lars's mother?"

"Yes. I just need to send one more text to my sister. The woman is insisting on instituting some new pastry with the supply chain the way it is right now. But she is the oldest and thinks she knows best. Like the place would even be the spot it is without my marketing skills—on top of baking most mornings, too."

"I'm sure that is frustrating, but Lars."

"Has been through this before, Doctor."

The cold statement made him want to slap the phone out of the woman's hand. He was pretty sure her son had a peptic ulcer, something less serious than cancer, but still serious. And she was fighting over text!

"I don't think his cancer is back."

"So an overreaction."

"Put the phone down and listen to me." He saw one nurse turn his head, but Syver didn't look away from Lars's mother.

Looking up from the phone, she opened her mouth, likely to yell at him, then realized who he was. Sometimes being a royal doctor had its perks.

"Prince Syver."

"At the hospital, I prefer Dr. Bernhardt, but yes."

"Lars will be so happy to meet you. He wants to be a doctor."

"He mentioned that." Syver took a breath, trying

to grant his patient's mother some grace. He didn't know what the argument with the sister was over and honestly didn't care. His focus, and hers, for the moment at least, needed to be Lars.

"The good news is that I think the anemia is the result of an ulcer. I am going to send you home with some recipes that will help balance his stomach acids until the gastroenterologist can fit him into her schedule."

Syver took a breath but didn't want to wait for her to say something or look back at her phone. "I will set up a consult with Dr. Holm, our oncologist, as well. Lars needs to be keeping up with his regular checkups."

"Thank you for the information."

Hazel slid from the room. "Lars was hoping you'd wait with him while Dr. Bernhardt fills out the discharge papers."

Her cell dinged, and it took all his patience not to roll his eyes as she looked at the text.

"Never go into business with the family. It always gets messy." She tapped a quick reply, then pushed through the door.

"I gave Lars my email address." Hazel whispered as they stepped away from the door. "I told him I'd forward questions about medical school and the process to you."

"You could have given him mine, Hazel."

"Syver, you are a prince. I am not dropping your email into a teenager's hands, or anyone else's, for that matter. And if his mother got it. That family business sounds like a nightmare."

"All family businesses have their difficulties." Syver tapped out a few things on the tablet that forwarded his consult requests and initiated the discharge papers with directions for a bland diet.

"Sometimes the best thing to do is drop the family." Hazel let out a sigh and leaned against the wall.

"You don't mean that."

The green in her eyes flashed under the fluorescents. "I do. You are not required to keep toxic people in your life. Cutting my mum off was best for my mental health—I don't regret having no contact with her. I waited too long to see the signs, but they were there and I acted. It was the right move."

The look he'd seen in her eyes was back. The challenge, the acceptance, the statement that if she'd done it so could he.

"Hazel." Meg raised a hand as she walked over. "We've got a set of twins in triage with coins up their noses. Help me with the extraction?"

"And that's my cue." Hazel hit his hip and wandered off.

Syver watched her, his blood cold. He knew her mother hadn't wanted her. Knew their relationship wasn't ideal, but the idea of cutting off family, of going without contact. What if she asked him to do that with his family?

She wanted to…he was nearly certain.

He was overreacting. He was tired; the first night on night shift always took adjustments.

She'd recommended he move out of the palace. But she was the one hesitating on the penthouse. Hesitating on his family.

The royal family was far from perfect. He understood that. But cutting his family off wasn't an option. It simply wasn't.

And Hazel isn't asking me to.

Not yet.

CHAPTER TWELVE

"ERIK CALLED."

Hazel didn't put a smile on her face as she looked up from the oven. "Asking after the penthouse again?"

Why was the King so insistent on them taking that offer?

Syver wanted to believe that by him stepping away from the palace, his brother was finally seeing his worth. Hazel's view differed.

She thought the royal family knew his worth. That was the problem. The people liked Syver. He worked among them, treated their children, offered smiles and everyday greetings.

That wasn't possible for the King and Queen, at least to the extent that it was for Syver. They wanted to use his connections. Give the royal family a facelift. Which would be fine if they wanted the changes to be more than surface level.

If Syver was the face of modernization, fine. But if he was simply a bright Band-Aid to hide the rot…

She'd been that Band-Aid once. She hadn't realized it with Alec, even though the signs were obvious once she stepped away. The signs she'd ignored. The pretty girlfriend who worked in healthcare… he couldn't be scamming the health facilities.

Hazel had no interest in playing that game again.

Even though she worried she was ignoring signs again.

She wanted Syver to have a genuine family. One that loved him for him, not for what he could bring them. She could be that. She was that.

"Are you going to tell me what he wanted?" The hesitation bothered her. Their relationship was great, except for the tension regarding the royal family. Tension she wasn't sure how to alleviate. Tension that was pushing its way into all aspects of their lives lately.

You are dating a prince.

"He says he has a surprise for us. At the penthouse."

"I still like the cottage better." She shook her head, trying to clear the complaint out. This was an ongoing discussion, but not the point of this conversation.

She took a moment, then asked her question, doing her best to hide the agitation. "What is the surprise?"

"If he'd told me that, it wouldn't be much of a surprise."

Well, that was true.

His arms wrapped around her; his lips pressed against her neck. "He invited both of us."

Leaning against him, Hazel pulled his warmth to her. This was her safe space. Wrapped in his arms, it felt like they could tackle anything…but his family.

She wanted to be as excited as he was. Wanted to see the positives, but Syver was grasping at breadcrumbs. They were a couple. Why shouldn't she just be included? That was the expectation, not a prize to be won.

She bit back the words, but they tore through her soul.

"When are we supposed to go?" She brushed her lips against his. If only the connection they had wasn't hiding behind their individual wants... and fears, now.

It had seemed so easy. So natural for them to slip from friends to lovers. They'd been like one. Now, though, they were drifting. They both knew it, but how did they fix it?

And should I?

Her soul shook at that thought. Syver was her person; she didn't doubt that. But she wasn't sure it was enough. She'd been so burned by Alec. She wouldn't do that again.

"Now...well, as soon as we get dressed."

Hazel looked at her overalls and bit back the retort that her comfy overalls were nice enough for the cottage. This was important to him. "I might need to *invest* in a few more nice clothes."

She meant the words to sound funny, but Hazel knew the exasperation was obvious, too. She didn't have the budget, or inclination, to spend money on "royally appropriate" clothes.

"I can always help if you need it."

"I don't." The words came out too fast, and she hated the flinch passing over Syver's face. "I just mean, I…"

Syver stepped in front of her. "I love you."

A sob caught in the back of her throat. It was exactly what she needed to hear. "I love you, too." They'd get through this tension, figure out their place in the royal family together. "We're a team, right?"

"Of course." Syver kissed the top of her head. "And if you want to wear the overalls, do it. I love anything on you, though I love you in nothing more!"

She unhooked the straps of her overalls. "We could always say it took us a while to get dressed."

"You are too tempting!" His lips trailed down her throat and for a moment, the world, its problems and all their expectations slipped away.

Syver's cell dinged for the fourth time as they approached the parking garage for the penthouse. "Are you sure you don't want me to check that?" He'd rebuffed her previous attempts, probably because it was the King, or the protocol office or something.

She'd considered texting Signe, asking if there was an issue she should know about. She and the Queen were getting on well, but she didn't want to pull Signe into any drama. The woman was making the best of the life she had, and was seven months pregnant. She didn't need any additional worries.

"I'm sure Erik just wants to know where we are."

"Maybe the delay wasn't the best idea."

Syver reached for her fingers, pulled them to his lips, then pressed a kiss to her palm. "I wouldn't change that delay for a second. Though I don't feel like explaining it to my brother either."

"Signe is pregnant—I suspect he'd understand."

"Erik only understands the crown." Syver's words were so soft, she wasn't sure he'd meant to speak them. "We're here, now. So he'll see us shortly."

Syver leaned over, kissed her cheek, then sighed. "I appreciate you agreeing to this. I promise, we are not committing to the penthouse, at least not today."

She'd scheduled another showing for the cottage. A place she figured was only still on the market because it was her and Syver looking. The Realtor had called in a favor to put it on hold while they discussed it, and the seller had agreed. Something they couldn't continue to do. It wasn't fair.

Syver slid a key card into the elevator, and the option for the penthouse lit up. Security was nice, but they worked with the public every day. And the residents of Fönn had given them space in their private lives.

Hazel didn't want to live in a gated community or in a high-rise where she had to have a special key card to gain access. She wanted to live some place that was theirs. A place no one could yank away.

A place where they didn't have to perform. A place where she wouldn't worry about expectations, if she was meeting them, or look for signs of something going wrong. No place the palace offered could ever give her that.

The doors of the elevator opened, and camera flashes immediately started.

"What!"

"Syver!" King Erik's voice sounded over the clicks.

Syver dipped his head toward hers, an act that she was sure would look lovely when the photographers were going over the snaps later. "Smile—act like we knew."

His breath was warm against her ear as he slid his arm around her waist.

Hazel's bottom lip was shaking. She wanted to scream, wanted to hit the buttons on the elevator and return to the garage. Go back to her little flat, get into her overalls or comfy yoga pants and pretend they'd told Erik they needed more details, or they weren't showing up.

Instead, her feet followed Syver as he moved toward the King. Someone had furnished the place. There were even a few pictures of them together at the baby shower.

God, it looked like they already lived here.

"We're here to announce, publicly, Prince Syver's relationship with Ms. Hazel Simpson. The palace is thrilled these two are happy and moving into this penthouse. Prince Syver's work at the hospital has kept him from participating in many royal engagements."

Syver stiffened as the lie fell from his brother's lips. He took part in everything asked of him. The royal family just hadn't asked much of him.

"However," Erik raised his arm, gesturing in a rehearsed way, that looked off. Like he was preparing to toast Syver. Had he rehearsed this speech with a champagne glass that he was now missing? "On my mother's suggestion, I plan to make him the face of my health and family initiatives."

They'd kept the imposter heir away, but now that he was more popular than his brother, now that the people of Fönn showed Syver preference, he was important.

It wouldn't last.

"And of course, we plan to have Ms. Simpson by his side." Erik met her gaze, daring her to argue.

The words clawed at her throat, ached to escape as she stared at the man who was using his brother, a man who only wanted to be part of his family.

Then he looked at his brother. "I suspect we'll be having a royal wedding soon."

A royal wedding. The thing Syver had never expected to get. Erik had given the man she loved everything he thought he wanted.

But it wasn't a genuine offer.

More camera flashes went off as questions spilled from the lips of all the gathered journalists.

"Syver." She wasn't sure he could hear her quiet plea, but she wanted away from here. The crown had trapped them.

The hint about the royal wedding was as good as a proposal. And none of it was for them.

Her eyes met his, and her heart sank. Syver's face was brilliant. He was getting what he wanted, finally. The imposter Prince made real by the brother who'd used him but never made him family.

And he could yank it all away if Syver didn't perform. If she didn't perform. "Syver, we have to talk now." The words were quiet, but she saw the female journalist to her side raise a brow.

"Syver." She grabbed his hand. "Please."

"I think my love is a little overstimulated. If you'll give us one moment."

Erik's face fell for an instant before the King threw a pleasant mask back on. "Ms. Simpson isn't quite used to this. But she will be."

They moved to the master bedroom, and Hazel wasn't shocked to find it empty. "So the palace only decorated the public areas for this ambush."

"I know it feels like an ambush, but sweetheart, Erik is offering me," Syver shook his head, "offering us a place, an actual place, in the royal family."

"Is he?" Hazel crossed her arms as she moved to look out the window. "Because weeks ago, he held us hostage in the palace because he thought I spread information about the Queen. Ignored us completely when you moved out. Then that stupid poll came out showing that you are the most popular royal, Syver…"

He had to see this, he had to, for what it was. A ploy to make sure the King controlled the narrative. He was giving Syver what he wanted, but it wasn't real, if it wasn't honest.

"He can take this away as soon as his image is rehabbed, or if you do something wrong, or if I do. We don't need this."

"I need my family."

What am I?

Pain echoed across her thumb as blood trickled into her palm. She'd pulled at the skin, not realizing how tender she'd made the flesh.

"They need you. But you don't need them. You don't." He was owed more than an ambush, more than a sliver of acceptance.

"I'm never going to cut my family off, Hazel. Yes, we have our differences, but they are my family. I know you did it, but I can't. I won't give up on them."

Words hurt. She'd always known that, but she'd never thought they could break her. "Is that what you think I did? You think I gave up on my mother?"

"If she reached out tonight, would you take her call?"

"No." It was the truth. If her mother reached out now, it would be because of Syver. Not for her.

His jaw clenched as her truth landed between them. "Sometimes you have to look past the failures of others. Meet them where they are. Not everyone can be perfect. I choose to look past their faults, to accept them for who they are. Even if they aren't what I want them to be."

She'd made each of those excuses once, too. Tried so hard to believe that she'd find a way to be enough for her mum. Maybe marrying a prince would do it. But if the only reason her mother wanted her was because of who she was dating or married to…well, Hazel was enough without that.

"I choose me. Maybe that is selfish, but I tried my entire life to be what she wanted, whatever that was. An outstanding student, a nurse, a woman living with a wealthy man. Nothing was good enough."

She held up her hand. She needed to get these words out before her heart finished shattering. "If she wanted me, *for me*, she could have me now. If she reached out, and I believed she wanted me. Just me. It would heal a torn part of my heart that will never feel full without her."

"And you think Erik doesn't want me for me?"

Hazel could see the hurt. And the determination. This was what he wanted. Pain ripped through her soul.

She'd seen all the signs this time. Knew he wanted his family most, and she'd overlooked them. Hoping that his family might give him what he wanted. But it was Syver doing the bending…and it always would be.

She took a deep breath, took in his face, reached

for his hands, knowing it was the last time she'd hold them. She wanted a Pause button, a Rewind machine that let her go back to this afternoon. Relish his touch.

If she'd known it was his last, she'd have memorized every soft kiss, every brush of his tongue, every touch. "What I know is that I love you, for you." She put her hand on his chest, knowing the tears were streaming down her cheeks.

"But I also know that isn't enough. You want…" She gestured to the closed door and the illusion of acceptance that was behind it. "You want his attention, acceptance. I can't fill that hole for you.

"I won't have my home or my job threatened because I don't follow a script. He just basically announced our engagement—you haven't asked me—we haven't talked about it. Not seriously. Syver…"

"I mean, I love you. He's just putting the royal stamp of approval on us."

And that was the issue. The heart of all the tension. He needed the stamp, and it was the last thing she wanted.

Her eyes slid to the door, then back to him. "I can't walk this path with you, but I hope it is everything you want it to be."

"Hazel."

Lifting on her tiptoes, she pressed her lips to his, then pulled away.

"Good luck, Prince Syver."

* * *

She was gone. And yet everyone had continued on. Acting like nothing was wrong. That this was just another royal engagement, another random party or announcement made by the palace.

It was like the reporters hadn't seen Hazel step out of the unfurnished bedroom, tears streaming down her face, head held high. Hadn't asked her questions she refused to answer as she left. Even to the most untrained eye, it was obvious they'd fought.

Fought.

That word indicated there was a chance. A way to patch things up. He'd chosen his family. Made it clear he wouldn't lose them. Made it clear he *couldn't* lose them.

So he'd lost her.

The world had shifted forever.

Yet, the night moved on.

Unlike Syver, Erik's tongue wasn't tied. He'd changed the topic, made an excuse for Hazel, like he knew her. Transitioned the night to the palace's priorities. Because he was the King, the audience he'd used for the "surprise" followed his lead.

Which was good, since there was no way to vocalize all Syver's thoughts. No descriptors to place on the magnitude of hurts, nothing but mental anguish at the breaking of his soul.

Reporters weren't owed that coverage.

"I think that went well."

Syver couldn't stop the hurt chuckle from breaking through. "Well? Well! You ambushed my girlfriend and I."

"Ambush is such a petty word. You and Hazel were not moving fast enough. You moved out of the palace almost a month ago. I offered you this place two weeks ago."

Just after the poll came out.

Hazel's voice echoed in his mind. And the voice wasn't wrong. The timing was suspect.

"It was a nice offer. I appreciated the palace thinking of me." *Remembering me, choosing something for me.*

Erik rolled his eyes to the ceiling before wandering to the kitchen and grabbing water from the fridge. "Living in a little place, it looks bad. Mother agrees."

He knew their mother agreed, but that didn't make it true. "It is not that small." It was a nice flat. They just needed something bigger, something that was theirs.

Ours.

His heart broke as he looked around the penthouse. It was nice, better than nice. It was elegant, with lots of lights for plants…plants Hazel would never bring here.

"The point is, the palace needed action."

"Action?"

Erik ignored the interruption. "We'll plan a wedding in, say, December? Holiday themes are always brilliant."

"Wedding?" Syver shook his head. "How can you possibly think the woman who walked out of here in tears will meet me at the altar under your order?"

Only the fury building in his chest allowed those heartbreaking words to escape. Hazel would not meet him at the altar. Erik had seen to that.

He'd made his choice. His family. He'd serve as the head of Erik's health and family initiatives. Two things incredibly close to his heart, but there'd be no wedding.

Is it worth it?

Why was his brain offering that question now? He'd made his choice. The palace was finally seeking a place for him. Bringing him into the royal family, truly.

"A hissy fit." Erik shrugged. "Signe's had them before, too."

Hissy fit. It was a good thing Hazel wasn't here to hear the words. She'd launch into him. And Syver almost wished he'd get to see it.

"I have things I need to do tonight, Erik." Like gather his things from Hazel's, try to move forward with the life he'd chosen. Make peace with his choice. "But before I leave, I want to run a few things by you regarding the health initiative."

"Mother suggested you, but you were my choice. It's yours to run."

My choice.

Warmth flooded his system. He was his brother's choice. Words he'd never said, likely never thought. Syver was right; his family could change. Could accept him.

"That's good to hear. We need to focus on recruiting medical professionals. Many professionals that left during King Eirvin's reign—"

"Father did his best."

Erik's interruption didn't surprise Syver, but he would not react either. King Eirvin hadn't focused on all of his subjects. He'd reserved his kindness, his affection and his favorable decisions on those he liked best. Those with access to stroke his ego, to make him feel big. Something most of Fönn had no opportunity to do.

Whether his brother wanted to admit it or not, the former King's focus on the aristocracy had driven many people to other opportunities. Students seeking to study abroad rarely returned. It was a deficit he wanted rectified.

But that was not an argument he wanted to have this evening.

"If I can convince doctors, nurses, techs to return, maybe other professions will follow, too." That was the easiest initiative.

"Do what you need to do. I don't need to be involved."

"Don't you want to be?"

Erik pulled his phone from his pocket and sighed as he flipped through a few messages.

Syver's stomach rumbled as he watched his brother. The health initiative was near and dear to his heart. He'd lobbied for control, or at least input, since the moment he landed on Fönn. His brother had finally chosen him.

But what if he'd only chosen him to keep him close now that he was pulling away? Syver had expected to be an integral part of the conversation for years, only to be rebuffed. What if he'd never been allowed close because Erik didn't want him around, even for projects he didn't care about?

Those were poisonous thoughts…

Only if they aren't true.

He needed to focus. Tonight was a lot. Too much, but right now, he needed to focus on what he had, not what he'd lost.

"As far as the family initiative…" His tongue felt like it was plastered to the roof of his mouth. What did he know of family? He'd lived apart from his, metaphorically, if not physically, for most of his life.

Children needed secure environments. Needed to know their needs, physical and emotional, were met. If they weren't…

If they weren't…well, many people ended up in a cycle of chasing admiration. Doing their best to make their families happy without ever gaining success. The trauma produced often lasted a lifetime.

If she wanted me, for me, she could have me now.

Hazel's words echoed in his mind. She'd been born in conditions so opposite from his. Her life growing up had produced trauma, knowing she was unwanted.

Unwanted...

Being born with a literal silver spoon in your mouth didn't protect you from that. Class didn't matter if your family didn't want you.

"Did you offer this flat because the poll showed I was more popular than you?" It wasn't the conversation they were meant to have, but the words refused to stay buried.

"What does that have to do with the family initiative?"

That wasn't a refusal. Redirection was a skill they learned just out of the cradle at the palace. Get asked something uncomfortable, redirect. Usually the person won't even notice.

"Nothing, and everything, if you think on it. Our family isn't exactly functional."

His brother laughed. Laughed.

The sound was so cruel after everything he'd done for the royal family. He'd bent himself into their mold—and now, now his brother, his king, was laughing. "It's not a joke."

"Of course it is. Syver, you aren't even royal. Or at least you shouldn't be. If Mum had had more control—"

How long did this argument have to play out?

Erik was just over forty, and Syver would turn thirty-five this year. This family history did not need rehashing. It was buried, in more than one way.

"There is enough blame to lie at both of our parents' feet, but I never asked for this. The thing you control least in this life is who you are born to."

"You're right. You've done nothing. You weren't in charge of anything. You work for a living. *You* left the damn country!"

Sent away...not left. Syver wasn't dragging those semantics into the argument.

"But the country loves you best. Explain that!" Patches of red coated Erik's face and water spilled across the counter as he slammed the bottle down.

The fury on Erik's face tore the mental cushions Syver had always placed around his family. The cushions that let the mean, cruel, insensitive and terrible things bounce off him. Let him take the hits they'd delivered.

The dam broke. The cord severed...just like Hazel said her relationship with her mother was. He'd been willfully blind.

"So all of this," he gestured to the penthouse, to the documents Erik had held up earlier showing he was in charge of the health initiatives, "it's because I was the most popular royal in some stupid poll?"

"Those polls matter, Syver. If the royal family isn't popular..."

Syver waited for Erik to fill in the blank space of his statement, but he just fumed.

The quiet tore through the flat. "This isn't the age of executing unpopular royals. The problem is the crown hasn't acted for the everyday people in years. If ever."

"How dare you!"

Syver shrugged, the chains he'd wrapped around his controlled responses dropping away.

"It would take so little to please people. Focus on the health initiatives, the emigration issues, family, poverty—you could bring so much aid to those areas. Issues the people care about, issues I've championed without the royal family's support.

"That's why I'm liked. Because I care. Not for the gain, just because it is the right choice."

"And that popularity is why we offered you this chance."

We...not I. My mother is choosing duty. Indirectly, not that it matters.

Duty would always come first. Hazel was right. Though part of him had known that hours ago. Weeks ago...his whole life. He just hadn't wanted to admit it.

"If I don't perform the way you want, what happens to the penthouse?"

It didn't matter; he would never live here. But he needed to know just how blind he'd been.

"Why wouldn't you perform?"

That was a punch in the gut.

Erik didn't even consider it a possibility that he

wouldn't fall in line. That he wouldn't jump at this chance.

He'd always done what was asked of him. Even when it hadn't gotten him any affection, any love. He'd stayed in London, he'd stayed out of the way in the palace, kept himself out of the spotlight. And none of it had ever been enough.

Looking at his brother, he saw their similarities. They had their mother's bright blue eyes, her full lips, but Erik bore the broad nose of his father. And his personality was King Eirvin's, too. Whether that was because he was in his father's shadow, because of genetics or a combination of the two, Syver didn't know.

They bore some of the same DNA. But genetic material did not make a family.

"I have no intention of performing. No intention of acting the part anymore." The words were freeing. His body was light as he let go of what he'd wanted for so long.

"Syver!" Another way Erik and his father were similar. But the sharp tone, hovering on disappointment, no longer made his insides curdle. "Walk out that door, and I will strip your title from you. Strip your family. Mum will stand by the royal family."

She would. He knew that, and it didn't change his mind.

Syver looked at his brother and sighed. "You can't strip something I never truly had."

Erik opened his mouth, but no words left, and Syver wasn't waiting any longer.

He was free. Something he should have been years ago.

Better late than never.

"Good night, Your Royal Highness."

CHAPTER THIRTEEN

THE WORLD HAD lost its color. Rationally, Hazel knew it wasn't true, but her entire body ached as she stepped through Meg's front door. She'd walked from the penthouse suite, wandered through darkened gardens for hours before finally texting and asking Meg if she'd come get her and let her crash on her sofa.

At some point, Syver was going to come back to their flat, and she was too cowardly to see him tonight.

"You going to tell me what's going on?"

Hazel shook her head. Even if she wanted to, she wasn't sure she could get the words out.

After losing her home, her career, her country following Alec's crimes, she'd sworn she'd never let others decide her destiny. Promised herself she'd look for any indication she was in danger of losing her heart, of having her life turned upside down.

Falling in love with royalty wasn't in her plans. But she'd done it and lost at love again.

Her body was hollow.

She'd made the right choice, hadn't she? Syver wanted to impress his brother, wanted to belong.

Was that so bad?

She was not traveling that path. She'd made excuses before. Hung on and lost everything.

Except it felt like she'd lost more than everything

this time. What was a home, a career, even a country compared to her losing her heart?

"Tea?"

Hazel nodded as she fell onto Meg's sofa. The overstuffed blue couch enveloped her as she pulled into herself as much as possible.

"I only have green tea." Meg passed her the mug. "Probably should have mentioned that."

"It's fine, Meg." Green tea might not be her favorite, but at the moment she was looking for warmth. Fönn was chilly at night, but Hazel didn't think she'd ever feel warm again.

"My fiancé is out tonight."

Hazel flinched at the term fiancé. She'd thought she and Syver would meet at the altar. Not with the royal blessing, but just as themselves. One day.

They'd not discussed it, but it felt like that was where it was heading. Hell, even the palace had seen it.

A Christmas wedding.

She didn't want to make the palace happy, but being married to Syver by the end of the year… Her bottom lip trembled, and she lifted the mug to her lips, knowing the tears were going to spill over again.

"Did I ever tell you why I came to Fönn?" Meg crossed her legs and continued before Hazel could offer anything.

"My ex-fiancé left me at the altar. Literally. I was standing in my poofy white dress with wilted roses looking at a door I knew he wouldn't walk through."

Hazel blinked, not sure what to say. Meg was the happiest person she knew. And thrilled to be engaged—even though she'd clearly done it once before to tragedy.

"Yet, you're marrying Lev."

"*Yet*, I'm marrying Lev." She held up her hand, admiring her ring. "I ran from Maine—I mean, I flew, but...well, you know. I had no plans to find love again. In fact, when Lev asked me on a date, I turned him down. Told him I wasn't interested in dating, period. And he told me to let him know when I changed my mind.

"No pressure, no additional asking me out. Nothing. He was just there. And I realized that if I let fear drive my future, I'd never find happiness. Not really."

"Fear can keep you safe." Hazel closed her eyes, hating the words she'd said, but hearing the truth in them, too. She hadn't listened to her gut before... and it had cost her everything. "The royal family..."

"Is a bit much." Meg winked. "But Syver is different. It's why everyone likes him."

"Everyone does." With a few exceptions. His family tolerated him, and she...her feelings were much deeper than admiration.

"He's still processing his family," Meg offered.

Hazel felt her eyes widen at Meg's words. "What...? Why...? Um..." It wasn't her place to talk about Syver's family, or how much he wanted them to love him. A task she didn't think they'd ever be up to.

"One benefit of marrying a historian is you learn all sorts of facts."

If Meg wanted to distract her with history facts now, Hazel wasn't really in the mood. "Meg—"

"His name starts with an *S*. Did you know that on Fönn it was common for bastards to be given *S* names before the turn of the nineteenth century?"

She hadn't. And she hated how much it made sense. She'd been an unwanted child. Named for the color of her eyes. And his family had followed an ancient tradition.

"So the whole country knows?"

"No, but they suspect. Whoever it was, the royal family covered it nearly completely. If they'd given him a traditional name..." She sighed. "He was gone for a while, banished, though it's not discussed. He's almost broken away. Leaving the palace to live with you, dating a commoner, he's leaving and they're grasping, trying to pull him back. But it won't work."

Hazel couldn't stop the laugh. "Don't be so sure."

Meg hadn't seen the need in his eyes tonight. Hadn't seen the desire, the craving. It was a hole she couldn't fill, a tear she couldn't patch. She knew that, because the hole in her soul was still there, too.

"You didn't see him before you came. Whatever happened tonight, it won't matter. He's seen them for who they are. Maybe he isn't willing to admit that yet, but once you see it, you can't unsee it."

"So what, I just wait? I just hope that one day he chooses himself? Chooses us without conditions or the hope that his family will swoop in?" The words tumbled out, and the tears poured over her cheeks.

"I can't tell you. But living in fear that it will never happen…" Meg's mobile rang, and she looked at it and held it up. Syver's number was clear on the screen. "Want me to answer?"

"No."

Hazel held out her hand, and Meg laid the mobile in it. "I'll be in my room."

Pressing the Answer button, Hazel pulled the phone to her ear. "Meg! Do you know where Hazel is? I'm at our place, and she isn't here. We fought and her phone goes right to voice mail. I need to find her, please."

"I turned my mobile off" Her voice was quiet, but she knew he heard her.

"Sweetheart, I know I don't deserve trust right now, but I'm asking. Meet me at the cottage."

"It's nearly midnight, Syver. It's late, and we've had a bad day, and…"

"I know. I know all those things. And you're right, but meet me at the cottage, Hazel."

"How would we even get in? Asking the Real-or…"

"I called in a favor. Say you'll come."

Fear wanted her to say no. Wanted to throw up

the walls she'd put around herself so well. But her heart refused to utter the words.

"All right. I'll be there shortly." Hazel blew out a breath as she hung up the phone.

"Road trip?" Meg was smiling as she leaned against the doorway.

"It's late. I can hire a car."

"Absolutely not. Let's go, Princess!" Meg grinned.

Hazel shook her head. "Not a title I'll ever have."

"Good. Titles are dumb, but I'm still calling you Princess!"

Hazel didn't have the strength or will to argue, so she just followed Meg to the car.

The cottage didn't have furniture. He'd bought a few plants on his way here, and hung some tiny lights to give them some ambiance. The heat wasn't on, but it felt like home. Or it would, once Hazel was here.

He'd called in a favor, one of his last acts as Prince Syver. Gotten the keys from the Realtor on the promise that he'd close on the cottage by the next week.

His mother had sent a text. A text...a short missive asking him not to try his brother. It was always him bending. Never them.

He didn't doubt the threat from his brother. The title would vanish, his limited access to his family would evaporate, too.

There weren't words to describe the hurt tha

caused. However, it didn't change his decision. He had his own life. Something he was proud of.

Now he just needed the woman who held his heart.

A car drove up the gravel path, and Syver blew out a breath. He needed Hazel more than anything. Letting her walk away this evening was a mistake he wouldn't repeat.

Opening the door before she could knock, Syver hated her red eyes and puffy cheeks. He'd hurt the woman he loved, because she saw him for who he could be. He'd spend the rest of his life making sure she never felt that again.

"Hazel." The urge to reach out to her, to pull her close and never let her go crawled through him. But he wouldn't rush this.

"Why are you out here?" She stepped inside, but didn't touch him. "At this time?" Hazel looked around the cottage, her eyes catching the plant holder in the corner and the lights.

"I talked to the Realtor. Promised we'd close on the cottage by next week, and she agreed to give me the keys."

"Benefits to being a prince." Hazel swallowed and clasped her hands. "Sorry, I didn't—"

"You did. And you're not wrong. There are benefits to a title. I figured I may as well use them one more time before it's stripped."

"Stripped." Hazel shook her head. "No. That is not fair."

"I thought you didn't want me beholden to my family?" Maybe it wasn't a fair question, but she'd seemed so certain this afternoon.

Her nose twitched. "I want them to want you for you."

"Well, I don't think that's possible."

Hazel stepped forward but stopped before she reached him. "Syver…"

"You were right. It's not me, not really, that Erik wants. It's an image, a reflection, one that I'm never going to fully meet."

"I'm sorry." Hazel reached for his hand.

Her warmth centered him. "It's me who needs to apologize, sweetheart. You were right, and I threw some horrid words at you earlier. You didn't give up on your mum. You just stopped letting her control you."

"It hurts to do." Hazel squeezed his hand. "It hurts a lot. But it was the right action for me."

It burned. That was the best description he could give. A heat pressed into his heart, a longing for a world he craved, but doubted would ever be in his grasp.

But that didn't mean he couldn't have a loving family. A family that would choose him, just him. "I can't describe the pain. Not yet. But I know that it's nothing compared to the pain of losing you. You're my family, Hazel. Now and always. I will do whatever it takes to convince you of that. However long it takes, but you and the life we build together are the family I choose."

"Wow." Hazel stepped into his arms. "Those are the sweetest words you could ever say to me, Syver."

"Because they're true." After pressing his lips to the top of her head, he sighed. This was his place. Beside this woman, creating his own path in the world, rather than trying to follow someone else's.

"I wish it hadn't taken you leaving, or me pressing my brother. I wish I could have seen what must have been so obvious to you. I know it was only hours ago, but it feels like everything shifted."

"Because it has." Hazel lifted up and kissed his cheek. "I also wish I'd stayed. I wish you hadn't had to press him alone. I let fear that you'd never see what he was doing drive me out. I let my fear, my past, drive my reaction, too. I regretted it as soon as I left. I love you, and I promise, whatever path we create, we do it together."

"Together." There was not a better word in all the world.

Together.

EPILOGUE

THE BELLS OF the church rang, but it wasn't for Hazel and Syver's union. She was a holiday bride, though Christmas Eve was still a week away. However, there was no royal regalia, no international press corps.

Erik hadn't formally stripped Syver's title, but he no longer used it in any form. The palace gates were sealed to him like they were to all citizens without an appointment. His life looked very much like any other doctor's on staff at the hospital.

And it was perfect.

But it meant instead of standing in the giant church in the middle of the capital city, she was in the hall of their cottage. Dressed in a red wedding dress with a white faux fur coat over the top, ready to meet the man she loved more than all the world in their backyard, with just the friends they saw as their family.

There was no other place she'd rather be.

"Rethinking getting married with snow on the ground?" Meg dabbed a tear from the corner of Hazel's eye. "You'll mess up your makeup."

"No, I'm not upset about the snow. The makeup, well, I was always going to meet him with happy tears on my cheeks." Happiness coated every fiber of her being. She'd never thought it possible to love and be loved so well. And her eyes refused to stop their joyful watering.

"Well, I'll be in tears too, though I blame the hormones." Meg ran her hand over her very pregnant belly.

The music started and Meg handed Hazel her flowers. "Here we go."

Here we go.

Hazel waited for Meg to reach the makeshift altar they'd put in their backyard. Light snow was falling, but her body never felt warmer. She was marrying Syver.

Her best friend.

The "Bridal March" started, and she almost raced to the altar.

After reaching for her hand, Syver kissed her fingers. "I thought brides walked slowly down the aisle."

She didn't try to stop her giggle. "I could blame the cold, but the truth is I didn't want to wait." She knew her smile was brilliant as the officiant offered a small cough.

They turned in unison, without dropping their hold on each other. They were entering the next chapter in their story of forever, the same way they did everything else.

Together.

* * * * *

*If you enjoyed this story, check out
these other great reads from
Juliette Hyland*

Redeeming Her Hot-Shot Vet
Rules of Their Fake Florida Fling
The Prince's One-Night Baby
The Vet's Unexpected Houseguest

All available now!